MW00980028

SUSPICION
ISLAND

SUSPICION ISLAND

Jeni Mayer

Thistledown Press Ltd.

© 1993, Jeni Mayer
All rights reserved.

Canadian Cataloguing in Publication Data

Mayer, Jeni, 1960-

  Suspicion Island

  ISBN 1-895449-00-6

I. Title

PS8576.A866S87 1993 jC813'.54 C93-098030-1
PZ7.M386Su 1993

Book design by A.M. Forrie
Cover illustration by Iris Hauser
Typeset by Thistledown Press Ltd.

Printed and bound in Canada by
Hignell Printing Ltd.
488 Burnell St.
Winnipeg, MB R3G 2B4

Thistledown Press Ltd.
668 East Place
Saskatoon, SK
S7J 2Z5

Acknowledgements

Edited by Peter Carver.
This book was published with the assistance of
The Canada Council and the Saskatchewan Arts Board.

For my father,
who knows where the winged ones sleep,
and my mother,
who dreams among them

PROLOGUE

The misty shadow of a dream drifted away as the telephone rang shrilly in the night. Daniel opened his eyes and groaned. A shaft of moonlight shone through his open bedroom window. The warm prairie breeze was richly scented with smells of freshly mown hay and damp earth.

"Someone gonna get that?" he called in the dim light. But his query was met with silence. There was not even the rustling of blankets from his parents' room next door. Again, the phone rang.

Still languid with sleep, he swung his feet onto the floor and stumbled to the living room. He found the phone in the near darkness, nearly dropped it, then brought it to his ear.

"Hello," he croaked.

"Is that you, Daniel?"

"Who is this?" He could barely hear over the pops and hiss of static.

"It's me . . . Grandpa."

"Hey, Gramps, how're you doing?"

A series of blips and squeaks filled the line. Daniel pressed his ear tighter to the phone and tried to make out his grandfather's reply.

"Don't come to the island!"

"What's that?" Daniel asked, certain that he must have misunderstood.

"Stay away!"

"Is this some kind of joke?" He shouted to be heard above the static. It was now so loud that his grandfather's reply was nothing more than a muddled string of unconnected words.

"Stay away . . . danger . . . mustn't come . . . Suspicion Island."

The line went dead. Even the static had stopped, replaced by an ominous silence.

Daniel stared at the receiver in his hand. His grandfather had invited him to spend the summer at his new home in the Gulf Islands off the coast of British Columbia. Why would he renege on the offer at the last moment? It didn't make sense at all!

The last time he had spoken to his grandfather was more than two months ago. Harold Christie, a well-known mystery writer, had only recently returned from a two-week jaunt in Tibet. He had sounded so excited about the island and had invited Daniel to spend the summer there with him and his new wife.

What was the meaning of this strange call? Daniel pondered as he switched on a nearby lamp and dialed his grandfather's number in the dim light. But there was no reply, just a steady endless buzz in his ear.

"Who's on the phone?"

Daniel spun around. His mother was standing in a strip of moonlight, with her hand resting on the back of the sofa. Her black hair stood out at odd angles, and a woolly housecoat cloaked her to the knees.

Looking at his mother was like looking at a mirror image of himself. They had the same shoulder-length black hair and deep green eyes. Even their angular noses, wide, full mouths and dimpled chins were identical.

The irony of it always made Daniel want to laugh. With the exception of their looks,

Daniel and his mother were not at all alike. They were like two opposite sides of a coin.

"I thought it was Grandpa," Daniel replied, then shut his mouth tight. He didn't want to give his mother another reason to refuse to let him go to Suspicion Island. She and Gramps hadn't got along since the death of her mother more than fifteen years ago. She was always complaining about Harold Christie's wild ways. And his grandfather's recent unexpected marriage to a thirty-six-year-old photographer had only added fuel to the flame. His mother was now certain that Gramps had finally gone completely off his rocker.

"And . . . " She looked at him questioningly.

"It . . . it wasn't him after all. I guess it was just a wrong number . . . " Daniel set the phone back on its cradle and tried to smile convincingly at his mother.

She took a step closer and gave him a pleading look. "It's not too late to change your mind about going."

"Don't start with that again," Daniel moaned. They'd been over this a hundred times already. "You know I wait all year long to spend the summer with Gramps. I can't wait to see him."

"I know that!" His mother looked pained. "But things aren't going to be the same. I just don't want you to get hurt."

"What d'you mean by that?" Daniel tried to keep his voice even.

"It's not just going to be the two of you any more. His wife is going to want to spend time with him too."

"You make it sound like he's just gonna throw me out like an old shoe." Daniel felt uneasiness creep over him.

"That's not what I'm saying." His mother drew her fingers shakily through her hair. Her lips were pinched tight. She looked equally tired of this same old argument. "It's just that Grandpa isn't going to be able to devote all his time to you any more."

"His marriage isn't going to change a thing!" Daniel spit out, clenching his fists at his sides.

"Of course it will. And if this *woman*," she said the word as though she were spitting out poison, "is worth her weight in salt, she'll put a stop to your grandfather's crazy antics: flying off to every god-forsaken place in the

world . . . acting like he's eighteen years old .
. . diving out of airplanes."

"Same old song," Daniel muttered under
his breath. "I'm going back to bed." Why
couldn't his mother see that Gramps thrived
on adventure? Why did she always make it
sound like he was some kind of lunatic?

He flung himself across the bed and
studied the shadows the moonlight created on
the luggage that sat packed and ready by his
door. He tried to force his mother's words
from his mind, but they refused to be denied.
"Things aren't going to be the same . . . the
same . . . the same."

And rising above his mother's words was
his grandfather's warning. "Stay away from
the island . . . danger . . . ."

1.

Daniel Bentley gripped the seat of the water-taxi as an unexpected wind shot across the ocean. The boat swayed to the left, then settled down to a gentle roll. A sense of uneasiness settled over him as he squinted out the window at a blanket of clouds building in the east. They hung dark and heavy, threatening to unleash torrents of rain.

"What in the world have I gotten myself into?" he grumbled, recalling his grandfather's late-night warning.

He glanced nervously at the boat's skipper, Captain Morrison, who had treated Daniel like a leper ever since he'd come aboard. He answered Daniel's questions in single syllables and refused to meet his gaze.

The man was sheathed in a dark grey rain slicker, though the twenty-six-foot launch was closed in. The hood was pulled up, almost obscuring his craggy face. Here and there a lock of white hair peeked out. He seemed unaffected by the mounting storm.

Daniel shivered as the captain glanced back at him, and their eyes locked. The old man half smiled, half sneered, then turned away.

Daniel let his gaze drift along the western horizon. The sun was beginning its descent into the ocean's depth. Fingers of light transformed the sea into a wrinkled sheet of pink and orange stained glass.

He was assailed with an overwhelming sense of confusion. On the one hand, he could hardly contain the anticipation of seeing his grandfather again. They had spent the summers together as far back as Daniel could remember. And each summer was an adventure, whether it was para-sailing over Skaha Beach, studying the tiny marine life that inhabited the wave pools on the west coast of Canada, or salmon fishing on the northernmost reaches beyond Anchorage, Alaska.

But his mother's words still stung him. Would things be different now that his grandfather had remarried? Would his grandfather be so taken with his new wife that he wouldn't want to spend time with Daniel? He loathed the jealousy that rose inside him, and he fought to get it under control.

"Welcome to Suspicion Island." The captain's voice snapped Daniel from his thoughts.

He looked at the island looming on the horizon. It loomed out of the ocean like a phantom. The highest point seemed to rise from the centre, and then the land fell away until it met the beach. Most of the island's features were hidden beneath the blackening sky and the shadows created by the boat's dim light. It was only the revolving beacon from a lighthouse on the eastern tip of the island that cut the gloom of the night.

Daniel squinted in the near darkness as a crack of lightning brought the island to life beneath its violent glare. For a few seconds, the light reflected in the windows of a tall two-storey house that was perched on the hill. Its outline was momentarily etched in the sky, then suddenly vanished.

The image was frightening. It looked like a house out of a horror movie. The eastern side of the hill it sat upon sloped steeply to the shore. To the west, the hill took an abrupt and drastic drop into the sea. The house rested perilously close to the cliff's edge.

Daniel hugged his coat closer to his body and checked the fastener on his life jacket for the tenth time. His fingers were now adept at finding the tiny catch in the dim light.

The impending storm seemed to recede into the background as Daniel thought of his grandfather's phone call. As he replayed the strange warning, his apprehension returned.

Water splashed through the boat's open window and splattered his clothes. The chilling cold snapped him out of his thoughts. He shivered, then gave himself a mental shake, trying to brush off his bleak thoughts. Maybe the phone call had been nothing more than a bad joke . . . or a dream. Besides, it was too late to worry now. The boat was rapidly approaching the island. A rickety wooden dock was now only a few metres away.

As the craft pulled alongside the dock, Daniel was immediately struck by the gloomy appearance of Suspicion Island as the captain killed the boat's engine. The beach was vacant. The thick trees and underbrush surrounding the shore cast swaying shadows on the sand.

"Do you think they're home?" He leaned forward and peered out the front window. There were no lights shining from the house on the hill. It looked abandoned as its high pitched roof reflected the light from the revolving beacon, then fell into relief.

"Gotta be. Ain't no way off the island 'cept this boat."

Daniel rose, suddenly eager to get his feet back on solid ground.

But, as he stood, the boat shifted with a rising wave and pitched him back onto his seat. He steadied himself, stepped more cautiously to the back of the boat, then outside onto the dock.

The light from the boat illuminated the sandy shore. But there was no sign of his grandfather. Beyond the beach a tangle of vegetation hugged the ground and huge trees towered over all.

Where is he? Daniel wondered, studying the desolate beach.

As though reading his thoughts, Captain Morrison spoke. "It doesn't look like the old man's comin' for you." He stepped from the boat and secured it to the dock. He reached into the open deck at the stern and gripped Daniel's duffel bag. He flung it carelessly at Daniel's feet.

"Doesn't my grandfather have a boat of his own?" Daniel asked as he bent to retrieve the bag. He looked across the sand to a set of long winding steps that led up through the dense growth toward the house on the hill. He swept his hand nervously through his hair.

"Yeah, but it's just a little wooden rowboat. He ain't fool enough to take it out on a night like this." Morrison looked pointedly up at the darkening sky. "Besides, the island is surrounded by currents. His little rig wouldn't stand a chance in 'em."

Daniel shifted his gaze. There was no boat tied to the dock or pulled onto the shore. "Then where's his boat?"

"He keeps it over on the north side of the island." The older man bent to reel in the length of rope that secured the boat. "Best fishing in the area."

Daniel flinched as a chill wind swept across the water. The trees surrounding the beach rustled.

"Couldn't one of the other boats from your company have picked him up?" Daniel set his duffel bag down, then removed his lifejacket.

"Nope. Isn't any other driver that will even come to this place." Morrison slung Daniel's second bag onto the dock.

"Why not?"

"I guess most of 'em are just nervous." The captain lowered his voice to a whisper. "What with Crazy Old Jeb livin' here and all."

"Crazy Jeb?" Daniel's eyes widened. He recalled his grandfather mentioning that one other man lived on the island.

Morrison nodded his head, then gestured over his shoulder to the beach. Daniel turned his head and caught a flickering movement in the tangle of growth on shore. A solitary figure stood motionless in the trees less than three metres away. The man's long grey hair hung over broad shoulders and a scraggly beard hid most of his face. The rest of his features were obscured by leafy dappled shadows. He looked large and menacing in the diminishing light.

"What's he doing there?" The hair on Daniel's neck rose.

"Waiting for his supplies." Morrison leaned over and retrieved a box from the back of the boat, then set it down on the dock. "He'll stay there in the bush until we both leave."

Daniel looked over his shoulder at the unwavering figure. "Jeez," he muttered. Jeb looked like a ghoul amid the trees.

"Oh, he's harmless enough," the captain said. "Just a little strange. Lives off the land . . . never leaves the island or has any company . . . don't take kindly to outsiders. You know the kind!"

"Not really." Daniel's turned to face the shore and gave a start. Jeb was gone. The trees wavered in his absence. Daniel's flesh prickled.

"Don't you worry about him. Ain't nothin' but a harmless old man. Just a little loony, that's all."

"Sure. No problem." Daniel gave a short, nervous laugh. The sounds of the island began to press in around him: the waves breaking loudly on shore, then receding, the wind howling through the trees, the wooden dock creaking and moaning in rhythm with the sea.

"Look, if I'm going to get to the mainland before the storm hits, I'll have to leave right now." Morrison pointed overhead to the bulging black clouds.

"Well . . . okay . . . if you really have to."

"You just go on up to the house. I'm sure your grandaddy just fell asleep or forgot you were coming today."

Daniel looked uncertainly up at the shape of the house on the hill. It looked menacing and unnaturally dark.

"What about his wife, Maria?" Daniel asked. "You'd think one of them would have remembered I was coming."

The captain's face took on an odd cast. The light in his eyes winked out and his voice grew cold. "Your grandaddy's wife went to the mainland this afternoon. Hired me special for a big photo shoot she had in Vancouver." Morrison's hands rapidly coiled the anchor rope.

What was it that Daniel saw in the old man's eyes? Contempt? Anger? Why did the mention of Maria cause such a strong reaction? What did Daniel know about his grandfather's bride, anyway? Who was she? Where had she come from?

He turned back to study Morrison, hoping to understand what it was that he saw in the old man's face. But a mask had fallen over the captain's wrinkled features. His smile was forced, his lips narrow and bloodless.

"See you in a week." Morrison quickly changed the subject, then looked away. "Watch out for Old Jeb!"

Daniel flinched. "Hey, I thought you said . . ."

"Oh, don't pay me any heed. I'm just teasing." The captain laughed — a laugh that somehow did not ring true.

"Yeah, right," Daniel muttered. Some joke!

He bent and swung his duffel bag over his shoulder, then gave a curt wave. The boat's engine raced to life, then the craft pulled away from the dock and set off.

He retrieved his other bag, then peered into the trees. Jeb had not returned. The shore was once more vacant and still. He looked down at the box of supplies marked "Jeb Palmer", then back up at the building cloud bank. He shook his head. If the old man wanted to leave his supplies to get rained on, it wasn't his problem.

He trudged across the sand, then up the narrow tree-lined path beyond the beach. Thick shadows followed him as he ascended the staircase that meandered up the steep hill. Rumbling thunder drew nearer and lightning flashed overhead.

A strange whispering sound swept through the trees. It had a human quality, like the murmuring of voices.

Daniel hesitated as the whispering grew louder around him.

"Grandpa, is that you?"

" . . . that you . . . that you?" His own voice echoed back at him. He broke into a breathless run up the stairs.

2

Daniel paused to catch his breath as he reached a large flagstone landing at the top of the hill. The house stood silhouetted against the sky beneath the roving lighthouse beacon.

The tall house was a series of curving arches and sharp peaks, all covered with latticework that was overgrown with a blanket of silver ivy. Several narrow posts held up an awning that led to an enclosed verandah. One of the posts was tipped to the left, transforming the awning into a droopy-eyed smirk. The house looked in dire need of repair.

The wind was building to a crescendo. It whistled as it raced past the latticework and screamed through the eaves like a host of angry cats.

Daniel took a guarded step forward, then reached out and rapped on the door. He waited several moments, but no answer came. Inhaling deeply, he tried the door. It was unlocked, so he drew it open and stepped into the verandah. The door slammed shut behind him with the force of the wind.

The house was quiet. There were only the muffled sounds of the wind and the distant waves beating on the shore far below.

"Hello. Is anybody home?" The narrow verandah was empty save for a wicker sofa, a chair and a potted plant that sat on a small table between them. The room smelled of geraniums and the electric scent of the storm.

Daniel took measured steps to the second door. It creaked as it swung open. Once again he called out. Still there was no reply.

He waited hesitantly as his eyes adjusted to the dimness inside. Dark shadows crouched motionless before him. He set his bags on the floor and began to search for a light switch. Stepping further into the room, he stumbled on something in front of him and tumbled forward. He heard an ungodly yowl as he landed with a thump on his knees. One splayed hand halted his forward motion.

He swore as an electric jolt of pain shot through his wrist, then he gasped. Two gleaming green eyes glared at him.

Summoning his courage, he pushed himself back onto his feet and snapped on the light switch. It illuminated the room in its bright glow.

"Cassandra," he breathed. "You scared me half to death." He reached down and picked up the large tabby cat, who was licking her wounded tail.

"I swear you're going to outlive me." His grandfather had taken the stray in more than twelve years ago. She had been carted around on hundreds of his grandfather's adventures. Cassandra had probably seen more of the world than most people ever hoped to.

The large cat, quickly bored with all the attention she was receiving, struggled free, then leaped up a set of stairs that led off to the right. Daniel laughed as he watched her scurrying along with the energy of a kitten. She disappeared into the shadows at the top of the stairs and Daniel turned to inspect the room.

He stiffened. He could hardly believe his eyes as he surveyed the chaos around him: furniture was overturned, lamps lay shattered on the floor, pottery vases lay in a broken heap.

"What in the world happened here?" He rushed out of the living room and into the next room. He snapped on the lights as he went.

He was greeted by another mess. The doors of the kitchen cupboards stood open. Several boxes of cereal and cans littered the counters. A plastic container and a broken jar of molasses were glued to the tile floor in a gooey heap.

Daniel stood motionless, trying to understand the clutter that lay before him. Finally, he turned and left the room.

He took the stairs two at a time to the second floor, hoping he'd find his grandfather sleeping peacefully, unaware of the havoc in the rest of the house. But he was filled with doubt.

The damage was equally apparent on the second floor. Someone had done a thorough search. Drawers gaped open with clothes hanging out. The blankets had been pulled from the beds and lay in tangled piles on the floor. The mattresses stood at crazy angles against the walls.

A small room that must serve as his grandfather's den was a disaster. The bookshelves that lined one wall had been stripped. Books lay scattered on the floor. Loose papers from a filing cabinet were strewn everywhere.

He stepped to the doorway of an adjoining room and froze. The contents of a darkroom lay scattered on the floor. Tables were overturned and a chair was smashed into a slivered heap of wood.

Daniel felt his airplane dinner souring in the pit of his stomach. Photographs were strewn around in disarray, and the room reeked with the odour of developing fluid.

Gradually his attention focused not on the destruction itself, but on the subject matter of the photographs that were scattered about. His grandfather's smiling face was captured in each frame. His hair had been cut fashionably short and his green eyes sparkled with delight. Had Maria taken these photographs? Daniel wondered, as an uneasy feeling grew in his stomach. How many times had Daniel seen that same childish delight on his grandfather's face?

It was almost as though the photographer had captured his grandfather's soul.

As his gaze wandered from photo to photo, Daniel wondered if his mother hadn't been right after all. Maybe Maria had replaced him in Grandpa's life! He ran his hand over his forehead, feeling moisture beading his brow. He turned and rushed from the room.

His feet felt like dead weights as he went back downstairs. When he reached the living room he removed his jacket, righted an over-turned chair, and flopped down into it.

With any luck his grandfather had been off the island when the destruction had taken place, despite what the captain had said. Maybe he had gone somewhere with friends. Maybe he was waiting for a break in the storm before returning home. Maybe someone had simply robbed the place while his grandfather was away. But as Daniel scanned the wreckage surrounding him, his hopes sank.

The house hadn't simply been robbed. He was sure of it. It looked as if someone was searching for something in particular. If it had just been a case of robbery, then the thieves had been rank amateurs. Several priceless paintings lay on the floor. A leather-bound first English edition of *War and Peace* was crammed against the wall.

Daniel and his grandfather shared a love of books. They spent hours every summer burrowing through second-hand book stores in search of old classics. The copy of *War and Peace* had been their greatest find ever. They had discovered it in a musty little book store in Vancouver and had bought the valuable dust-laden book for a song.

Fear and worry for his grandfather overcame him and he struggled to decide what to do.

He stood bolt upright as a thought struck him. "Phone for help." Daniel spoke his thought aloud. He was suddenly desperate to find an answer to this unsettling mystery.

Cassandra mewed loudly in reply as she sauntered back into the room. Daniel ignored the cat as he looked around for a telephone. It took several minutes before he located it beneath a stack of discarded books.

He lifted the receiver to his ear, then gasped. There was no dial tone. Nothing. The phone was dead. The line was silent.

He felt the room closing in around him.

He dropped the phone and bolted for the door, stumbling through the scattered debris. If only he could alert the supply boat captain before it was too late, before the boat sailed too far away . . .

As he reached for the doorknob, the lights overhead flickered, then went out. The clammy hands of darkness settled over him.

3.

Oh great!" Daniel snapped the light switch on and off several times uselessly.

Frustrated, he reached out and found the doorknob. He pulled the door open, then stepped into the verandah. The floorboards groaned as he moved to the next door.

As soon as he pulled the door open the wind and rain whipped into the room.

He wiped at the water that splashed in his eyes and looked out at the ocean below. His spirits deflated. A small light from what must have been Captain Morrison's launch bobbed far out from shore. Helplessly, he watched as the light finally disappeared in the shadows of the other nearby islands.

"Great!"

He turned and again stumbled through the living room. Stretching out his hands to feel his way, he found the chair he'd been sitting on and dropped into it with a sigh.

He drew deep breaths in an effort to ease his rising panic. He tried to relax his shoulders as he considered his predicament. He was stranded on the island, with neither power nor phone. His grandfather was missing, and someone had searched the house. But who were they, and what were they looking for?

He sank further into the chair, listening to the moaning wind outside.

There was nothing Daniel could do until morning. He would simply have to wait it out. There must be some clues to his grandfather's disappearance, something that would explain what had taken place in the house. But for now he had no choice but to wait. He could not search the house in the dark or the island in the storm.

He pushed a strand of hair from his forehead and tried to slow his breathing. Cassandra came out of the darkness moments later and curled up on his lap. He rubbed her fur. Her muted purr was a comforting sound in the night. Finally his body slumped and he drifted into a restless sleep as the storm raged outside.

Daniel awoke with a start hours later. His heart was pounding in his chest.

The storm had passed in the hours that he had slept. The wind had died down to a gentle breeze, the rain to a light shower. Even the sounds of the crashing waves far below had diminished.

Dawn was spilling light through the large windows into the living room. Several rugs were scattered about the highly polished wood floor. Their warm jade and sand shapes reminded Daniel of the paintings he had seen in the Indian villages he'd visited in Montana with his grandfather. The walls were painted the same jade green. Matching pottery lay scattered about in disarray. Despite the destruction, the room had a warm homey feeling. It seemed perfectly designed for his grandfather. There was a sense of the exotic in the design, something wild and untamed.

He stiffened when he heard a loud creaking. He sat forward in the chair and listened. The sound rose again — it was like footsteps on a creaky floor.

He strained to hear. Was someone walking in the verandah or on the landing out front?

"You're really letting this place get to you!" he scolded himself. The house was silent except for the muffled waves below. He stood up and walked across the room to a bank of windows that spanned one side of the long narrow living room.

The house had been built on the rim of the hill. The windows were precariously close to the edge. As Daniel looked down, he could see the sunlit beach beneath him. He stepped back several inches from the pane of glass and admired the coming dawn.

Cassandra padded across the floor toward him. She brushed her body against his leg, then plunked herself down on top of his feet. Daniel leaned forward and picked up the affectionate old cat.

Once again, he heard a loud thump. He set the cat down on the floor and walked to the front door. There was no denying it now. There was someone outside. The steady sound of footfalls was unmistakable.

Daniel felt an icy fear creeping into his belly. Was Crazy Jeb lurking on the other side of the door?

He flattened himself against the wall as the knob gave a rusty squeal, and the door slowly opened.

A unfamiliar figure stepped through the doorway.

Daniel heard a stifled cry, then realized the sound was coming from his own throat. Startled, the intruder spun around to face him. Their eyes locked for a split second, then the stranger jumped backwards.

Daniel didn't know what propelled him into action. All he could think about was preventing the interloper's escape. One moment he was staring at an unfamiliar pair of cold black eyes and the next moment he was lunging forward. The impact of his body sent them both tumbling to the floor.

He gave a startled yelp as teeth clamped on his forearm and his arm exploded with pain. He wrenched it back with a wounded cry.

The rising sun cast light on the face of the intruder beneath him and Daniel went rigid.

He stared back into the dark, angry eyes of a young native girl. Her cheekbones were high, and her eyes so black that they seemed to glitter with light. She looked the picture of innocence with her long, wet black hair tumbling around her shoulders. But the image was shattered by a string of profanities that she was hurling at Daniel, obscenities that he had only heard aloud in the locker room of his football team. Her eyes sparked with unchecked anger.

"Get off me, you pervert!" she bellowed, twisting her head toward his arm.

Daniel could still feel the burning sharpness where she had bitten him, and he struggled to hold her down. She lay screaming and squirming beneath him.

"Let's say you explain what the heck you're doing in my grandfather's house . . . then I'll decide whether or not to let you go!"

The girl stiffened, her mouth clamping shut, her eyes widening in surprise. "Your grandfather's house? You're Daniel?"

"Well, I'm glad you seem to know who I am. But that still doesn't explain who *you* are!" A grimace spread across her face as she began to struggle again. Daniel had her wrists in a steely grip, but she still managed to struggle free. She caught him with a stinging blow to the side of the head before he recaptured her arms.

"I'm Solano," she shouted as if that should explain everything. "Solano Wolf. Your *grandfather* is married to my *mother,*" she hissed. "Now get off me, you big oaf."

Daniel's arms slackened with surprise. She took advantage of the time to knee him expertly in the groin and send him sprawling onto his back in a spasm of searing white agony.

Daniel clutched himself and twisted onto his side. His breath came in fits and starts. A metallic taste rose in his throat. He lay shaking, waiting for the pain to slowly subside.

The girl who called herself Solano had risen and stood glaring down at him.

"You're . . . Maria's daughter?" Daniel choked out, his eyebrows raised in shock. He had imagined what his grandfather's wife had looked like a hundred times in the past months. But none of his imaginings had conjured up a woman of native blood. He wasn't really shocked by this discovery — only surprised.

"That's what I said, isn't it?"

"But you're . . . you're . . . " Daniel trailed off stupidly, not knowing how to voice his thoughts.

"Native!" Solano replied as though reading his mind. She flipped her long hair over her shoulder and scowled at him. "Is that what you were trying to say?"

"Not exactly . . . " Daniel lied. "It's just . . . it's just that Grandpa didn't mention that Maria had any kids, that's all."

"Well, now you know!" She turned on her heels as if to leave. Daniel struggled upright, ignoring the pain in his stomach, and gripped her ankle.

Solano spun around, her dark eyes flashing, and yanked her leg from his grip. "Look, macho man," she wagged her finger in his face, "in case you haven't noticed, we're on a friggin' island." She jammed her T-shirt angrily into her shorts. "Where the heck could I possibly run to?"

"Where's my grandfather?" Daniel ignored her sarcasm and rose on shaky legs.

Instantly, her fiery look disappeared. She stared down at her feet, blinking back tears.

"I don't know. I went out to pick wild blackberries yesterday after lunch. When I came back, the house had been trashed and Harold wasn't here. I went over to the other side of the island where he keeps his boat, but it was gone."

"And he hadn't been planning a trip off the island?"

"No."

"Maybe he just went fishing and couldn't get back because of the storm."

"He wouldn't have done that. He never would have left me here alone." There was such certainty in her reply.

"Just for a few hours?" Daniel queried.

"No!" Solano's reply was cold and final.

The answer startled and puzzled Daniel. Surely Solano was old enough to spend a few hours unattended. She must be at least thirteen. Couldn't she be trusted to fend for herself? Or was there another reason? Something more sinister?

"Was Grandpa acting strangely the last time you saw him?"

Solano paused and pondered the question. "Not really. He had been quiet, though, since Mom left for the mainland."

"Why? Had they been fighting?"

"Of course not. They're like two love-sick puppies." She rolled her eyes. "It was just like he had something important on his mind."

"Didn't you ask him about it?"

"Of course I asked! But he said it was nothing. Just that he was having trouble with the book he was writing."

"What was the book about?"

"How should I know?" Solano's eyebrows furrowed. "You must know how secretive your grandfather is about what he's writing."

Daniel nodded. He certainly was aware of his grandfather's strange quirk. He recalled how he had crept into his grandfather's den once, years ago, and had read the first chapter of his latest novel. He could still remember the angry look on his grandfather's face when he caught Daniel in the act. "Don't do that again!" was all his grandfather had said. But the anger in his voice was enough to convince Daniel to mind his own business when it came to his grandfather's writing.

He shook himself out of the past and looked at Solano. "Where were you all night?"

"I . . . I . . . thought whoever trashed the house might come back. I couldn't phone out for help so when it got dark I hid over in the lighthouse."

"All night long?" Daniel said doubtfully. He looked at her skimpy T-shirt and shorts.

A stony look dropped over her face. "Get off my case! I don't need a father!"

"Obviously your mother thought you did. Maybe that's why she got her claws into my grandfather!" Daniel barked, then instantly regretted it. Solano looked as though she'd been slapped. "Look, I'm sorry. That was a stupid thing to say. My grandfather never did anything in his life that he didn't want to do."

"Don't ever speak against my mother again." Solano's voice was ominous. There was a stormy look in her eyes.

"Jeez, I said I'm sorry." He felt colour rising to his cheeks. "What do you want? Blood?"

"Not right now." The corner of Solano's mouth twitched — half smile, half grimace. "Maybe later!"

Daniel considered her answer. Was this another warning? Despite her size, there was something threatening about Solano. Even her stance was defensive — as though she were ready to pounce at any moment.

"Look, why don't we get something to eat. Then we can talk more about this." It seemed useless to continue prodding her for answers. If Solano knew anything about his grandfather's disappearance, she wasn't about to confide in him — yet! "I make a great peanut butter sandwich," he offered, to lighten the tension between them.

"Yeah . . . right!. You'd probably poison it." Solano shot the words over her shoulder as she turned and stomped into the kitchen.

"Women!" Daniel muttered, following her.

They both paused in the kitchen doorway. Cassandra was crouched on the floor eating from an overturned bowl of cat food. She looked up at them, then turned away disinterested.

"I guess we'd better clean this mess up or we'll never get fed." He looked at Solano, wondering why his grandfather had never mentioned her. He watched her bend down to begin picking shards of glass from the gooey mess on the floor.

"Here, let me get that," he offered. "You'll cut yourself." He squatted down beside her.

Solano turned and looked at him sharply. "I'm quite capable of taking care of myself. I'm not an invalid!"

"Fine." Daniel rose and stalked out of the kitchen. "God, what a hothead," he muttered. He paced in the living room until his anger began to lessen, then stood in the doorway, studying Solano as she continued to work. Her body was extremely frail, even thinner than he had first noticed. Her face had a hollow look, her cheek bones jutting out starkly. And even though her skin was burnished she appeared unhealthy. Her eyes were red-rimmed and circled by dark smudges.

"How old are you, anyway?" The question was past his lips before he had a chance to stop it.

Solano looked up, startled. "Why do you want to know?"

"Are you always this defensive?"

"Only when my stepfather goes missing and my home is trashed."

Daniel nodded. "Look, I think we're both just a little too upset to think straight right now." He tried to keep his voice even. "Why don't we start over."

He extended his hand in a peace offering. Solano looked at it skeptically, then stood up and reluctantly grasped it.

"Peace," she said, then burst out laughing as she tried to release her hand from Daniel's grip. They were bonded together by a thick glob of molasses.

A healthy glow lit Solano's face as she laughed. Her eyes sparkled.

"I'm sixteen," she answered his earlier question through sputters of laughter.

"You don't look it." Daniel pulled their hands apart and walked to the sink. He too was sixteen but she looked years younger than he did.

"Don't remind me," Solano replied. "I spent half my childhood in the hospital. I think all that lousy food stunted my growth!"

"What was the matter with you?" Daniel asked. Whatever it was she didn't look like she'd got over it yet.

Solano's eyes hooded over. She didn't appear about to answer him. Finally, after a heavy pause, she shrugged her shoulders. "A few broken bones . . . cuts . . . bruises. No big deal."

"No big deal?" Daniel's eyebrows rose. "You must have grown up in a tough neighbourhood. Is that where you learned to fight like that?" Daniel could still feel his gut protesting against her earlier attack.

Solano shrugged.

"Where are you from, anyway?"

"The Flathead Reserve in Montana," she replied.

"Does your dad still live there?"

"No." Solano's face went blank. She grabbed a damp cloth from the sink. "You'd better wash that stuff off." She pointed to Daniel's molasses-covered hands. The light in her eyes dimmed. They looked like two lifeless black stones.

Daniel smiled weakly, then walked to the sink and turned on the tap. Nothing happened. He stared at it in aggravation. It must be on an electric generator system, he thought, cursing the failed power.

As if someone had overheard his thoughts, the kitchen lit up in a bright glow of artificial light. Seconds later, water blasted out of the faucet. He scrubbed roughly to remove the molasses, then moved out of the way so that Solano could wash as well.

When she finished, she bent down and picked up a towel that lay on the floor. Drying off, she handed it to Daniel, then grimaced as she caught sight of the angry red teeth marks on his arm.

"Sorry about that." She wet the end of the towel and patted it on the small wound. "I always was a biter."

"I'll remember that." He took the towel from her hand. "I had a dog like that once."

Solano smiled sheepishly. "Why don't we forget about eating now? I'm not very hungry anyway."

"Me either," Daniel echoed. In light of recent events he didn't think he could force himself to eat. "I think I'll go down to the beach and see if there's any sign of Grandpa yet." He dropped the towel on the cluttered counter and turned to leave.

When he reached the verandah he paused. The sunrise lit the room in a beautiful kaleidoscope of colour. It shone through little rectangular strips of stained glass inset at the top of each window. Reds, pinks, and oranges colored the wooden floor of the glass-lined entrance.

He gazed out the window at the awakening morning, wondering what could have happened to his grandfather. The unanswered question hovered in his thoughts as he left the house. He shivered beneath the warm morning sun. Goose-flesh rose on his arms.

The thick forest that hugged the steep staircase was quiet as he descended. There was not even the chirping of a bird to cut the eerie silence. There was something unsettling about the quiet that nagged at Daniel. Something about it seemed wrong . . . abnormal. It was like being in a theatre when the lights were low but the screen was blank and silent.

He pushed the disturbing thought away. He suddenly recalled Jeb Parker on the beach the night before. He hesitated, scanning the thickness of the trees. If anyone was hiding there, they would be well concealed in the overgrown vegetation. He continued uneasily down the staircase.

As he neared the beach, the gentle lapping of the waves broke the unearthly quiet. The steady, rhythmic beat was comforting. Bending over, he removed his shoes and socks and stood barefoot in the sand, enjoying the silky warmth beneath his toes.

The goose-bumps that had covered his arms while he was walking down the path began to recede. The end of the raging storm last night had brought a sweltering day in its wake.

He scanned the horizon, taking in the beauty of the ocean and the other islands that loomed green and rocky in the distance. White-capped waves flowed towards shore, then receded.

He looked to the west at a huge outcrop of jagged rock that marked the end of the beach and extended out into the ocean. The jumble of stones, less than two kilometres down the beach, started at the peak of the hill and gradually declined until it reached the ocean. It served as a barrier that seemed to cut off the long sandy beach from the western tip of the island. Could the cove his grandfather had described over the phone two months ago lie beyond this rocky point?

He wondered fleetingly if he would be able to climb the rocks to have a look at the other side, but quickly pushed the thought away.

The climb looked dangerous. The promontory was shiny, slick from the pounding surf. The grey-black point glistened in the distance.

He looked back at the other islands and drank in their peaceful atmosphere.

The scenery looked much different than it had the night before. It was almost tranquil. The narrow blue-green strip of sea was calm. Several snow-capped mountains were scattered on islands along the horizon. It seemed ironic that just a few kilometres away there were telephones. But there was no way off Suspicion Island with the deadly currents that surrounded it. The phones might as well have been on another planet.

His serenity disappeared as he turned back to look at the house on the cliff and noticed some strange marks in the sand. Two shallow troughs cut into the beach. They began at the bottom of the steps and led across the shore to the water's edge. The track was smudged in spots beneath his own footprints, but still distinct. The lapping waves softened the markings near the shore.

As he studied the strange troughs he began to wonder if something had been dragged across the sand. He looked back toward the waves, then paused when he spotted something brown bobbing on the water's edge.

Daniel felt his chest tighten as he walked across the sand. His mouth went suddenly dry as he bent down and retrieved a sandal from the waves. It was one of a pair he had given his grandfather a year ago for his birthday.

4.

The isolation of the island began to close in on Daniel as he held the cold, wet sandal in his hand. Had his grandfather been dragged across the beach and flung into the sea? Had he been unconscious . . . poisoned? There were no signs of a struggle in the sand, just the narrow track of ridged wet sand.

"Stop it!" Daniel scolded himself. Maybe his grandfather had simply lost his sandal.

He plunked himself down on the beach and looked at the waves. His fingertips caressed the smooth, wet leather as he tried to make sense of the situation. There were so many unanswered questions. It was all so confusing.

He shifted around to look at the house on the hill. Why hadn't his grandfather mentioned Solano? Why had he kept her a secret for so long?

A shiver rippled up and down Daniel's spine. Sweat trickled down between his shoulder blades and his shirt stuck to his skin.

He turned to face the water again, trying to regain his earlier feeling of peace, but it was impossible. He couldn't force away his building confusion.

He rose, muttering under his breath as he put his shoes and socks back on. He gripped the sandal tightly in his hand and started toward the staircase. He took the steps two at a time, trying to ignore the heavy silence surrounding him.

He stood on the landing and looked around. The house looked less ominous in broad daylight, but the front door that stood wide open reminded Daniel of a mouth gaping in silent horror.

He followed a noise to the kitchen.

Solano was standing by the open fridge seemingly lost in thought. He remained silent, watching her as she reached out and grasped something in her hand. She brought a small vial near her face as though examining its creamy white contents, then caught sight of

Daniel. The colour drained from her face and she made a quick movement to hide the object. Daniel watched as she tried to palm the small vial with a shaky hand, dropped it to the floor, swooped down, picked it up and stuffed it into the pocket of her shorts.

It all happened so fast that Daniel nearly doubted what he saw.

"What are you up to?" he asked.

"Oh . . . nothing much." Solano turned her back to Daniel and began straightening objects on the kitchen counter. Her hands looked unsteady as she stacked and restacked canisters.

Why had she been in such a rush to hide the vial? What was the creamy substance that it contained? And more importantly, where had Daniel seen one just like it before? Weren't there similar vials in the pharmacy at home, lined up on the medication shelf at the back of the store?

"You recognize this?" He held his grandfather's sandal in front of Solano.

"It's Harold's shoe. Where did you get it?"

"I found it down on the shore. It looks like someone might have dragged Grandpa out into the water."

"But that's crazy. Who would do such a thing?" Solano's jaw was tight and her lips were pulled into a thin line.

"Got me beat!" Daniel said. "But I think we'd better try and get hold of the police."

"But how? The phone's not working. The supply boat won't be back for days."

"I don't know!" Daniel hissed. "I'll just have to think of something." His brows furrowed as he turned on his heels and stumbled out of the house.

He began to regret his hasty retreat the moment he stepped outside. He had no idea where to start looking for a way off the island or clues to his grandfather's whereabouts. He refused to even entertain the thought that his grandfather might have been spirited off the island or, even worse, dragged unconscious into last night's stormy sea.

But, despite his indecision, he wasn't about to go back in the house. He needed space to think, time to sort out his chaotic feelings.

Taking one indecisive look over his shoulder, he threaded his way down the staircase and onto the beach below. He decided he'd just wander around the island. Maybe he'd discover something that would help him piece together the mysterious puzzle.

He followed a narrow strip of beach around the western edge of the island, towards the rocky point.

Several times the sandy beach gave way to stony outcroppings and Daniel was forced to cross the slippery rocks. Further along, the steep side of the hill gave way to a thick stand of trees and Daniel had to walk amid them as the beach disappeared beneath heaps of rocks and tangled growth. The smell of sweet scented moss hugged the bush and narrow streams of light cast flickering shadows in the trees.

He had walked less than a kilometre when he saw a sandy stretch of shoreline ahead. He was about to slip from the coolness of the forest when he saw movement on the shore. He crouched down and peered through the trees.

Jeb Parker sat on a log less than five metres away peering out at the ocean. His long grey hair was held back by a narrow thong of leather. His face was hidden beneath a shaggy grey beard. He was dressed in a pair of ragged jeans and his chest was bare save for a thick mat of grey hair. His feet were encased in leather sandals.

Daniel hunkered further down. He could feel his heart begin to quicken.

"You planning on hiding in there all day?" The old man's voice rose above the sound of the water lapping on the shore.

Daniel paled. How had the man known he was there? He hadn't even turned in Daniel's direction.

He considered sneaking back the way he had come. He could hear his own heart beating in his ears. But instead he crouched still and silent, too terrified to move.

"Don't try my patience, boy." The old man turned and looked directly at him through the trees.

Daniel screwed up his courage and walked out from the safety of the bush.

"I'm Harold Christie's grandson . . . " he stammered, pausing on the edge of the trees.

"I know." The old man stood and faced him. Daniel was taken back by Jeb's powerful appearance. His shoulders were broad, his hands like large mitts. His eyes were slate grey and unemotional. "Your grandaddy and I have an agreement. I don't go to his side of the island 'cept to get my supplies, and he don't come to mine."

"My grandfather is missing," Daniel stated, willing his heart to slow down.

"Is he now?" The old man said the words without any hint of surprise. "Lots of strange goings-on on the island lately."

"What do you mean?"

"Place is dying." Jeb looked out at the waves, then returned his gaze to Daniel.

"Dying?" Daniel stared at the lush green growth behind him. The land was bursting with life. What in the world was the old man talking about? Maybe Captain Morrison was right. Maybe Jeb was as crazy as a loon.

Jeb stood staring silently at Daniel.

"So you haven't seen him?"

"Like I told you. Your grandaddy don't come to my side of the island." The old man sat down on the log once more and resumed staring at the ocean.

Daniel held his ground as anger overrode his fear. How could Jeb be so unemotional about his grandfather's disappearance? "Do you have a phone I can use?"

"No phone . . . got no use for one." Jeb looked Daniel full in the face. A glimmer of something like concern filled the old man's eyes. "You try your grandaddy's two-way radio in the lighthouse?"

"Two-way radio?" Daniel started. Why hadn't Solano mentioned it? Surely she must have known that it was there. Hadn't she said she'd spent the night in the lighthouse the night before?

"Yeah. The lighthouse runs all by itself nowadays, but your grandaddy got permission to keep the radio in there. Something to do with its being the highest point on the island. He uses it to order supplies when the phones are down. Which is most of the time!"

"He . . . never mentioned it," Daniel sputtered.

"Oh, well. You ought to be able to get a message to one of the freighters that goes by here every afternoon. They can let the authorities know about your grandaddy."

"I'll . . . I'll do that." Daniel was dumbstruck. He couldn't believe that his only ray of hope since arriving on the island just twelve hours ago had come from the man who had so unnerved him the night before.

"Island's dying!" Jeb said as he rose from the log and walked away down the beach.

Daniel watched him until he was nothing more than a small spot in the distance. He started back to the house on the hill. One way or another he was going to find out why Solano had kept the two-way radio a secret.

5.

Solano was sitting in the verandah when Daniel returned to the house. He was struck by the colour in her cheeks. The smudges beneath her eyes had diminished and her skin had lost its sallow cast. Had he only imagined her sickly appearance before? Or was it a trick of the bright sunlight spilling in the windows?

He pushed the thought away as he recalled Jeb's revelation about the two-way radio.

"I thought you spent the night in the light-house." he said.

"I did." Solano looked at him seriously. Her eyebrows rose in an arc. "So what?"

Daniel didn't reply. Instead he stared back at her.

"My god." Her eyes grew large. "There's a two-way in there." She made a motion to slap her own forehead. "I can't believe I didn't think about using it. I guess in all the confusion it just didn't dawn on me."

"I bet." Daniel glared down at her, trying to check his rising anger. "How do we get to the lighthouse?"

"I'll show you." Solano stood and walked to the kitchen.

"My, you've certainly been busy," Daniel remarked as he followed her. The kitchen counters and floors were shiny clean.

She didn't comment. It was obvious from her rigid back that Daniel's sarcasm had not gone unnoticed. He followed her out the back door and onto a path that led down the eastern side of the hill through a tangle of overgrown brush.

The noonday sun beat down on them. The snap of breaking twigs accompanied their every step.

Within minutes the narrow trail opened onto a small clearing at the water's edge. The lighthouse was surrounded by a heap of large boulders.

The narrow tower was majestic. It soared into the sky overhead, looking as though it had recently been given a fresh coat of paint. The bright white-and-red striped siding gleamed in the morning sun. The smell of fresh paint mixed with the salty sea air surrounded them.

Solano scrambled up the rocks. Daniel followed, cautious to keep his feet from becoming soaked in one of the many tidal pools. They were filled with hermit crabs, starfish and tiny shelled creatures.

He stood beside Solano as she threw back a small latch that held the door, then stepped inside. They mounted the steps leading to the top of the lighthouse.

Daniel was breathless by the time he reached the circular room at the top. Pausing to regain his breath, he looked out the windows at the ocean. The water below was a rich blue-green. Large chunks of land, the other Gulf Islands, broke up the horizon in stark green slashes. The sky above was an endless expanse of blue.

He turned and surveyed the room. A smile played across his lips as he saw a desk off to the right. A black two-way radio rested on its top.

"All right!" He rushed over to the desk.

His heart skipped a beat as he flipped several switches and the console lit up. The radio was operational. Reaching out, he picked up the fist-sized microphone that hung from its side.

He stiffened. The microphone came clear off its mooring. Someone had cut off the cord. It was nowhere to be seen. The microphone lay useless in his hand.

Daniel burst into a string of expletives. He wheeled around to face Solano, the microphone still clenched tightly in his fist.

"I don't suppose you know anything about this?" He shoved the mike inches from her nose.

Solano stared at him open-mouthed, outrage spreading across her face.

"Yeah!" she bellowed. "I planned this whole thing." Her hands were on her thin hips and her feet were planted firmly apart. "I destroyed the radio so I could be stranded on this island with you and Crazy Jeb."

With flaming cheeks, she spun around and stomped down the stairs. The room rang with her footsteps on the metal staircase.

"Great!" Daniel sputtered. The lighthouse trembled as the door below was slammed shut.

He hurled the useless microphone onto the desk and shoved his hands into the pockets of his jeans. He plunked himself down on the chair by the desk, staring blindly out at the ocean.

He felt as though he was trapped in a nightmare and couldn't wake up. Why had he accused Solano of sabotaging the microphone? Surely she wanted to find out what had happened to his grandfather as much as he did. Or did she? another voice in his head questioned.

He tried to block out the niggling doubt, but it simply wouldn't go away. No matter how hard he tried, he couldn't convince himself to trust Solano. Was it only jealousy he felt? Was Solano, like her mother, just another person who stood between himself and his grandfather? Or was she hiding something, some clue that would unravel the mystery surrounding his grandfather's disappearance?

And what about Jeb Parker? Was he playing a sick game of cat and mouse, sending Daniel on a wild goose chase to the lighthouse, knowing full well that the radio had been destroyed?

Finally, unable to put the thoughts to rest, he walked down the stairs. Their clattering ring seemed to break the spell that was engulfing him and he felt better.

The hot sea air surrounded Daniel as he threaded his way back up the hill to the house. Sweat broke out on his forehead and trailed into his eyes. He wiped at the moisture as the path blurred in front of him. Then his vision cleared and he rushed on, anxious to get out of the afternoon heat.

Solano was sitting at the kitchen table eating a sandwich when he arrived. He paused in the doorway and looked at her. She refused to meet his gaze. Instead, she studied the half-eaten sandwich in front of her.

"Look, I'm sorry I yelled at you," he apologized.

She said nothing, merely looked up at him as if he were a specimen under a microscope and then dropped her gaze to her plate once more.

"It's hard to believe that you're Harold's grandson." She stared up at him again. "He's so nice."

Daniel shifted under her accusing gaze. He wanted to spit out an insult, but couldn't force himself to speak. She looked so pathetically sad.

"We're both just overly suspicious," Daniel offered. "Maybe this place breeds suspicion." Perhaps that was part of the island's disturbing aura, he thought. "I over-reacted."

"No kidding!" Solano looked disgusted.

Daniel stared at a invisible spot above the fridge, shuffling from one foot to the other. "I'm sorry," he conceded. It seemed easier to try to keep the peace.

"Apology accepted," Solano said.

Her words served as a peace offering and Daniel joined her at the table. He took the seat across from her and tried to divert her attention as he slid his hand across the table, attempting to snatch the second half of her sandwich. She caught the gesture and slapped his hand away.

Daniel looked at her through half-closed lids and feigned a pout. He looked hungrily at her sandwich.

"Oh, have it." Solano laughed at his pathetic puppy-dog look. "Who could resist that face?" She slid the plate toward him.

"None of the girls I know," Daniel said smugly.

"Oh, lord! An egomaniac." Solano rolled her eyes in disgust.

"Me?" He cocked his eyebrows up and screwed his mouth into a devilish grin.

"Yes, you!"

Daniel tried to look wounded, but her clear ring of laughter would not allow it. He burst into a hearty chuckle.

They sat eating in silence, caught up in their own thoughts.

Daniel was pleased that the tension between them had suddenly evaporated. It seemed simpler to try to get along. "When someone hands you a bag of bones, make a pot of soup." His grandfather's favorite saying came back to him in a flash and a smile tugged at the corners of his mouth.

"What are you smirking about?"

"I was just remembering some of my grandfather's famous last words," Daniel replied with a grin.

Solano's peaceful expression vanished. Daniel bit his lip. His hastily spoken words hung in the air like a threat. "My grandfather's famous *last* words." It echoed off the walls.

6.

Daniel set his sandwich back down on the plate. His mouth felt dry and the food tasted like sawdust.

Solano sat across from him, wringing her paper napkin between her fingers. Their eyes met and held for several seconds, then Daniel looked away and let his gaze wander aimlessly around the kitchen. He finally broke the silence.

"Let's go check out the other side of the island," he suggested. He couldn't help thinking that if his grandfather had gotten stranded on another island in the storm, he would probably return soon. The storm had long since passed and the ocean was calm.

"Yeah, sure." Solano jumped up. She dropped her twisted napkin on the table and started for the living room.

He followed her silently as she walked down the steps to the beach. When they had reached the sand, she turned to the left and spread the trees apart, forcing her way into the thick bush. A narrow hidden path stretched before them.

"You go to the other side of the island quite often?" He looked at the matted trail that angled away from them.

"Yeah. Harold and I like to come here in the evenings." Solano pushed the overhanging branches out of her way. "Mom usually follows the beach, but we like this way better. It's very pretty."

"Yeah, beautiful," Daniel muttered as a twig snapped out of her hand and sprang toward him. It caught him on the face with a stinging slap. He rubbed his cheek and grumbled under his breath. Why did the image of Solano and his grandfather together send an uneasy feeling racing through him?

As the path widened the earth gave way to thick jade moss that lent a spring to their step.

Small clusters of wildflowers burst out of the mossy soil.

Most of the sun was blocked out by the towering trees overhead. Only fingers of sunlight filtered in, giving the scene a shady fairytale beauty. The air was cool and damp and filled with the sweet tang of greenery.

"This way," Solano called out as the trail took a ninety-degree turn. The passage ahead was a series of curves as it skirted the base of the hill.

"Does this take us to Jeb's side of the island?" Daniel asked, increasing his speed. Solano was disappearing around yet another turn.

"No. Jeb only owns the cove and the western tip of the island. This path follows the eastern edge of the island." She gestured to her right. The stark white of the lighthouse was visible through the trees. "We won't be going near Jeb's land."

Daniel nodded. He had already invaded Jeb's territory once. He didn't plan on doing it again. There was something unnerving about the old man.

Neither Solano nor Daniel spoke as the path narrowed again. They had to fight off the branches that seemed poised to snap at their hands and faces. They both moved cautiously, pushing the tree limbs out of the way.

It felt as though they had walked for hours along the hilly pathway before the trail finally opened onto a wide sandy beach.

Daniel squinted in the afternoon sun as he came out of the shelter of trees. He glanced at Solano who was shading her eyes against the sun's glare.

"This is where your grandfather pulls up *Maria,*" Solano informed him.

"Maria?" Daniel asked.

"Harold named the boat after my mother," she explained.

Daniel forced himself to smile. The mention of Maria's name sent jealousy coursing through him. He knew he was being childish. But he simply couldn't help himself. He had had his grandfather to himself for too many years.

"What's your Mom like?" Daniel asked.

"She's a lot like your grandfather. She likes to live on the edge. They've gone sky diving once and para-sailing at Skaha a couple of times since they met. Mom loves that kind of stuff."

"Gee . . . that's great. She sounds perfect for Grandpa." *Maybe too perfect,* Daniel thought.

He fell silent and surveyed the beach before them. The sandy shore was unmarred by any signs of life, except for two sea gulls fighting over a dead fish washed up on the sand. But there was no boat, only the expanse of vacant beach.

Solano flopped down onto the sand as one of the gulls got a grip on the small fish and flew out across the water. The second gull screamed in protest and streaked out after him.

Daniel sat down next to her and picked up a large sea shell from the sand. His fingers caressed the barnacle-encrusted surface as he watched the waves break on shore.

"Maybe his boat was damaged in the storm and he has to have it repaired before he can come back."

"Maybe." Solano looked doubtful.

Daniel guessed that a small rowboat wouldn't stand much of a chance in the rage of last night's storm. He turned and looked at Solano. Was she thinking the same thing?

"Did you notice how quiet it is on the island?" Solano asked.

"What do you mean?" Daniel crossed his legs and looked seriously at her.

"I don't know." Solano ran her fingers through her hair. "It just seems like there's never any sound except for the ocean and the wind."

Daniel felt a strange quivering sensation, recalling the heavy silence that had so unnerved him on his arrival. "It is kind of eerie, isn't it? I don't think I've heard any birds other than the sea gulls since I got here."

"Or a cricket . . . or a frog. Nothing!" Solano added.

"Maybe Jeb's right, after all."

"You talked to Jeb?" Solano's mouth dropped open.

"Yeah. He's the one that told me about the two-way radio."

"You ought to stay away from him." Solano looked away, her hands nervously playing with the hem of her shorts.

"Why's that?" Daniel was curious about her reaction.

"I just don't think it's a good idea. I don't think he's quite right, if you know what I mean." She looked at Daniel and smiled. "There was this guy who lived near us in Montana that reminds me of Jeb. He was a real loner. He lived on the edge of this mountain all by himself. Shot at anyone who came near his property. I use to hide in the trees at the back of his old shack and listen to him prattling on to himself for hours and hours. He talked about the craziest things."

"Weren't you afraid he'd shoot at you too?" Daniel asked.

"That was the least of my worries when I was a kid!" Solano's voice dropped to a mere whisper and she stood up. "Let's go back."

"What's the rush?" Daniel stood up, bewildered. "What could possibly be worse than being shot at?"

"You ask too many questions." Solano started back to the path in the trees.

Daniel didn't bother to press her. It was obvious from her departure that the conversation was over. Finito!

"Let's go back this way." Daniel gestured to the sandy beach that swung back towards the eastern side of the island.

Solano paused and looked back at him. "It takes a lot longer that way." She looked at her watch before adding, "It's almost five o'clock."

"So what? You got a hot date or something?"

Solano seemed to waver with indecision. She glanced at her watch, back at the beach, then at her watch once more. It was as though she were making some unknown calculation. "Oh, all right." She started down the sandy stretch of shoreline.

"This is your grandfather's favourite part of the island," she said as Daniel fell into step beside her. She made a big sweeping gesture to the ocean and the trees and the long endless strip of sand. "He says it is the only place in the world that you can be truly alone."

He remained quiet as she rambled on. He tried to imagine his grandfather sitting on the beach, or walking near the water's edge.

Solano's constant chatter and the lapping waves served as a balm, and Daniel began to relax for the first time since he had arrived on the island. He let her voice lull him out of his depression, pushing away his worry for his grandfather.

They walked for several minutes before Daniel spotted strange markings in the sand. He came to an abrupt stop.

"What's the matter?"

Daniel said nothing — he simply pointed at the peculiar pattern in the sand. A deep v-shaped groove began at the shore and continued up to the forest that embraced the beach. And where the mossy floor of the woods joined the beach, the ground had been ripped up as well.

It looked as if something large had been dragged across the sand, then up into the trees. It reminded Daniel of the two narrow troughs he had discovered earlier this morning, only these were much deeper. The strange track disappeared into the shadows of the underbrush.

Daniel started toward the trees. Without speaking, he followed the groove into the bush. Solano followed close on his heels.

He came to an abrupt halt when the track ended. He saw a large mound of moss and twigs that rose unnaturally out of the earth. It looked like a gigantic, fresh grave.

Solano froze behind him. Her hands were clenched into tight fists, and her face had grown pale.

He edged toward the peculiar mound. His hands shook as he cleared away several of the branches that covered it. He felt smooth wood beneath his fingertips.

He held his breath as he cleared away more of the pile. His hands froze in midair as the word "Maria" became visible on the stern of a small wooden rowboat.

7.

Daniel flinched as he looked at the black lettering. He glanced over his shoulder and saw that Solano also looked ashen. Was this the reason she had acted so strangely when he'd suggested following the beach back to the house? Had she been afraid that he'd discover the boat? But that was crazy! How could Solano possibly know about the hidden rowboat?

"Grandfather's?" he croaked.

"Yes," Solano breathed. "But he never keeps it over here. He always leaves it on the north shore."

Daniel cleared away more of the camouflage and inspected the boat. It was no more than fourteen feet long and looked almost new. The white paint was nearly unmarred except for a few scratches. The oars were hanging from a rack inside. Two life-jackets rested near a seat in the middle of the boat, along with a green tackle box with his grandfather's initials printed on it in red lettering.

Why would anyone want to hide the boat? Daniel wondered as he brushed his hair nervously from his face. Was someone trying to make it look like his grandfather had left the island on his own? Or was the hidden boat merely a diversion?

Once again, his thoughts turned to Solano. "I suppose you didn't notice this yesterday?" He folded his hands across his chest and waited for her reply.

"Of course not."

Daniel's face must have shown his disbelief. Her face clouded and she glared at him.

"God, you make me sick. You arrive on the island in the middle of all this chaos and start pointing fingers."

"Just how *am* I supposed to view all this craziness?" Daniel sputtered.

"You might start looking for answers instead of peeking around every corner for the bogeyman."

Daniel took a step closer to her and pressed his face close to hers. "Yeah, well maybe you're right. Maybe I've been looking so hard for the bogeyman that I couldn't see it standing right in front of my face!"

"What's that supposed to mean?" Solano bellowed. Her breath was warm and sweet on his face.

"You figure it out." Daniel stomped past her onto the beach. His hands were shaking and his skin was on fire.

At that very moment, he would have given almost anything to get off the island. But even that was an impossibility. The small boat, buried beneath the leafy shroud, was not built to withstand the treacherous currents surrounding the island. He was trapped.

A troubling headache began to pound just behind his eyes and he tried to calm down. Every part of his body ached with fatigue.

Solano was still standing motionless in the trees as he slowly walked back to the path they had followed earlier and began the long winding walk to the house.

The narrow footpath was quiet and lonely. There was not even the chirping of a bird to cut through the silence that seemed to envelop the surrounding woods. Daniel paused, suddenly startled by the deep silence. He recalled his earlier conversation with Solano. Struck by an uncomfortable thought, he crouched down and studied the underbrush. Where were all the creatures that should have been scampering through the verdant growth? He recalled the dead fish washed up on the beach.

Shouldn't the trees be ringing with the sounds of birds? The forest singing with crickets? He stood up, discomfort tightening his legs and arms. Was Crazy Jeb right after all? Was the island dying?

The shade of the forest, so refreshing moments ago, now chilled him to the bone as he resumed his walk.

The house was silent when he returned, which suited him just fine. "I could care less if she ever comes back," he fumed. He knew he was being paranoid. After all, what reason did he really have of suspecting Solano in the first place? But what about the little vial she'd tried to hide? The broken two-way radio that she'd forgotten to mention? What about her rush to get back to the house?

He was reminded of Solano's earlier cleaning spree as he entered the kitchen. The smell of lemon hung in the air. He opened the refrigerator and scanned the contents.

His stomach began to rumble as he made a sandwich and then slumped unhappily into a chair to eat. He hadn't really taken notice of the kitchen before. He scanned it with a curious eye. It echoed the native colours in the living room. The walls were sand with specks of jade. The cupboards were a bright forest green. A braided sweetgrass bough hung above the doorway like mistletoe.

Had Maria decorated the house to remind her of the home she'd left behind? Was she trying to retain a piece of her past even though it was no longer a part of her life? He searched for signs of his grandfather's hand in the decor but could find none. It was almost as if his presence there had been obliterated — wiped away like dust on a chalkboard.

"Jeez," Daniel muttered. Maybe Solano was right. Maybe he was peeking around every corner looking for a bogeyman. But what else could he do? He had no concrete evidence, no definite clue to explain the mystery surrounding the ransacked house and his grandfather's disappearance.

With that thought, he swallowed the last bite of his sandwich. He debated whether he should have a sleep, but it was only seven o'clock. Fatigue was pulling at the corners of his eyes and his body felt limp. But as he looked into the living room at the overturned furniture he forced the tiredness away, choosing to try to put the house back into some kind of order. Other than the kitchen, the rest of the house was still submerged in chaos.

Pushing up the sleeves of his shirt, he went to the living room and began to straighten up the mess.

He moved about the room hanging pictures, righting furniture and clearing away broken vases and pottery jars. As he worked, he was aware of the silence in the house. Solano had still not returned.

Daniel recognized most of the objects in the room. Unlike the kitchen, the living room was filled with his grandfather's presence. His favourite books and paintings were scattered about. Even his reading glasses lay beside an overturned coffee table. Daniel felt comforted by the presence of his grandfather's things.

Occasionally he came upon an unfamiliar piece — a crude pottery bowl with intricate geometric patterns, a photograph with unfamiliar faces, and little beaded hangings. As he held them in his hands, he wondered about his grandfather's bride. How had they met? Was it Maria's idea to move to the secluded island? Where was Solano's father?

By the time he had finished cleaning the first floor he was exhausted. He had just sat down in a chair to rest when Solano came in. She didn't seem to notice him as she started toward the stairs. She looked ill. The dark smudges had returned to her eyes and it seemed an effort for her to walk. Her chin was tucked into her chest and she seemed to be concentrating on each slow and laboured step.

Her face registered surprise as she glanced over the railing at the newly cleaned room. She saw Daniel, threw him a stony look, and continued silently up the stairs.

Daniel felt concern. Was she sick? Should he go see if she needed anything? He rose, sat down, rose again, then sat down once more.

Indecision made his thoughts skip back and forth.

He studied the darkness outside through the wall of glass, blocking out his worry for Solano. The sky was like a black satin sheet and the stars hung so low that they appeared to be suspended by invisible strings. The moon was a chubby crescent against the darkness.

He stood and hung the last of his grandfather's paintings, then glanced around the room. It looked peaceful now that it was neat and tidy. If only havoc didn't still reign in the rest of the house!

Exhausted, he dragged himself upstairs. He paused on the landing. Which room was Solano's? He noticed several doors. Moonlight spilled in through a bow window at the far end of the hall. A big rocking chair sat beside it and a little table with an overturned lamp rested nearby. A beaded hanging glittered in the window. Had his grandfather sat in this chair only days ago enjoying the warmth of the sun flowing in the window? He could almost imagine him there, his tall frame stretched out in the chair, legs crossed at the ankles before him, glasses pulled down to the edge of his nose as he peered over them to study the pages of his latest novel. If only he were still there!

Daniel felt the first pangs of real despair and his eyes stung.

He heard a muffled noise as he started down the hallway. The door to his right was closed and sound filtered out. Once again he debated whether he should check in on Solano, but he threw the thought aside. He was tired and he didn't want another argument to mar his sleep. He turned to the room on the left.

It was a disaster, but the mattress that was upended against the wall looked inviting. He walked into the room and tipped it over so that it fell on the bed frame with a resounding thud. Without undressing, he flopped down, tugged off his shoes and socks, then lay wearily, listening to the muted sounds of Solano moving around in the room across the hall.

He lay with his eyes half-closed and tried to command his arm to grasp a blanket that lay on the floor nearby. He fell asleep before his fingers reached its woven edge.

He awoke hours later, shivering. The moon was barely visible. It was hidden beneath a thick blanket of cloud. Rain was lashing at the window pane, swept up by the rising wind. The bottom of the window was open a crack and the damp chill wind whistled in.

He heaved himself off the bed. Closing the window, he scanned the darkness outside.

A flash of light drew his attention to the beach far below. It cast a pale glow on the shore.

The window faced the western tip of the island. The long rocky point on either side of the cove blocked his view of the water below. All he could see was a narrow strip of the cove's shore.

He squinted through the darkness, trying to focus on the strange light.

A jagged bolt of lightning lit the island. For a few seconds the outline of a shrouded figure on the beach was starkly revealed in its glare.

8.

Daniel stared at the figure on the beach, wondering who would be in the cove at this ungodly hour. The distance and the darkness made it impossible to tell whether the figure was male or female. From his vantage point, Daniel couldn't even see how the figure had arrived. If there was a boat anchored in the water, it was hidden by the huge rocky promontories.

He watched the figure move closer to the base of the hill, then disappear out of view. Even the beam of light winked out.

Daniel stepped away from the window and began pacing the floor. Moments passed before he looked out again, squinting through the rain-sprinkled glass.

The moon was emerging beneath a heavy bank of clouds. It sent an unearthly glow onto the narrow stretch of vacant sand.

Daniel lay down on the mattress, letting his thoughts travel aimlessly. Was Crazy Jeb given to taking late night strolls in the isolated cove? Or was there someone else on the island?

He tried to return to sleep, but it was impossible. He tossed and turned for ages before giving up.

He rose and walked to the door, stepping quietly across the hallway to Solano's door.

He listened intently. No sound filtered out. The knob rotated easily in his hand. He gave the door a gentle push and crept into her room.

He was immediately struck by a cold blast of air. The window on the far side of the room was wide open and the chilly wind was sweeping in, along with the drizzling rain. The long white lace curtains that framed it stirred like a ghost in the breeze. Solano was asleep on the bed, her legs and arms moving restlessly beneath the blankets. Her hair lay damp against her forehead, framing her face like a dank mop.

He rubbed his arms, trying to block out the chilling air, and padded to the window.

The floor was wet beneath his bare feet. He was standing in a small puddle of water as he reached out and pulled the window down. It thudded against the sash. Glancing outside, Daniel saw the verandah roof a short distance below the window frame.

All thoughts were forgotten as he was suddenly driven to the floor beneath the force of Solano's body. She crashed down upon him, her small fists pummelling his chest and face. Her damp hair brushed across his cheeks.

"God almighty!" he exclaimed, trying to scrambled from beneath her weight. "It's me . . . Daniel!" he shouted as he brought his arms up to protect his face from her blows, then grabbed her frail arms to prevent another attack.

"What are you doing here?" she screamed. "You scared me to death!"

"Get off me and I'll tell you," Daniel felt the blood rising in his cheeks. He felt foolish, pinned beneath her narrow frame.

Solano rose, swearing. Daniel got to his feet, thankful for the darkness that hid his flaming cheeks. He readjusted his clothes and his composure, then in stammering words tried to explain.

"I saw someone on the beach . . . " he sputtered.

"What's that got to do with your being in my room?"

"Well . . . ah . . . I just wanted to check and make sure you were all right."

"I bet!"

Solano put her hands on her hips and threw her damp hair over her shoulder with a flick of her head. "Why don't you just admit you don't trust me? You've been acting like I'm some sort of criminal since you got here."

"I have not." Daniel shifted uncomfortably. But he knew it was the truth.

"Yeah, right!"

"I don't know what I believe any more." Daniel lowered his voice to a whisper.

"Me, either," Solano snapped.

Daniel instantly felt ashamed. He really hadn't given her the benefit of the doubt. But the forgiving thought died the moment he looked back at the pool of water beneath the window. Could Solano have climbed out onto the verandah roof, then slid down one of the many posts to the ground?

He turned to face her, stiffening as he looked at her damp hair. Was it sweat from a nightmare? Or was it rain from a late night walk in the cove?

"Get out." Solano's voice brooked no argument.

"I'm going. I'm going." Daniel wheeled around and started for the door. A flash of silver caught his eye and he paused. He looked at a night stand that sat beside Solano's bed. For a split second he caught sight of something that made his mouth drop like a rock. A syringe rested on the wooden table and a small vial, like the one Solano had tried to hide in the kitchen, sat nearby.

"Get out!" Solano screamed and stepped into Daniel's line of vision. Their eyes met and locked for several seconds. Had the darkness only created the objects that rested on the night stand? But the question, like so many others, went unanswered. Solano blocked his view as he walked shakily from her room.

9.

The house was quiet when Daniel awoke the next morning. After dressing, he started down the hallway, then paused at Solano's room. The door was wide open and the bed was empty. He immediately recalled the syringe and vial that he had seen the night before. But the table was empty save for a book, a half-eaten orange, and a glass of water.

He let his eyes wander over the room. He was certain that he had imagined the whole thing as he studied the cheerfully painted yellow walls. The hardwood floors shone in the light. A lemony flowered blanket lay crumpled at the end of the bed. The darkness, the storm, and the eerie figure on the beach the night before had probably sent his imagination into overdrive.

Daniel's attention was drawn to a jewelry box that lay overturned on the floor. He peeked out into the hallway. The last thing he needed was to get caught snooping. When he was certain that he was alone, he knelt before the little box. He righted it, then began sifting through the small heap of glittering metal. Most of the necklaces and earrings were cheap costume pieces. There was a collection of small sea shells, a polished stone, a colourful feather, and a handmade beaded bracelet. Tiny birds and intricate shapes were carefully beaded onto the leather thong in glimmering shades of azure, jade and red. Had Solano made this herself? He could almost imagine her sitting on a hill somewhere like an Indian princess, her hair dancing in the wind, as she attached each miniscule bead.

"Jeez!" The beautiful image startled Daniel. The last thing he needed now was to start having *those* kinds of thoughts about Solano.

He concentrated on sifting through the contents of the box. From beneath the pile, he retrieved a small photograph. Solano was smiling tightly for the camera, her white teeth gleaming, her shoulder draped by a muscular arm wearing the same beaded bracelet that

Daniel had held only moments ago. The man's face had been cut from the photograph. There was only a jagged hole where the features had once been.

Daniel dropped the photograph back onto the floor and picked up the bracelet once more. He slipped it onto his wrist. It was far too large and trailed halfway up his forearm.

Who was the man in the photograph and why had his face been so ruthlessly excised from the picture? Why did Solano now have the bracelet that he had once worn? Was it a gift taken back in anger? Or had she received it as a gift of love from the person in the photograph? Something akin to jealousy stirred in his belly.

The mystery surrounding the damaged photograph prompted Daniel to recall one of the novels his grandfather had written and he felt a cold chill. *Flashback*, the novel was called, and in it a serial killer had collected photographs of his victims and cut their heads out of the pictures before stalking them for the final kill.

He tried to return the contents of the box to its former disorder. He left the room feeling uneasy. He seemed helpless to stop the horrible images that were building inside him.

Solano's face was set in a tight, unreadable mask when he arrived in the kitchen. She didn't raise her head as he sat down in the chair opposite her. She didn't look like she had slept well at all. Her eyes were red-rimmed and her mouth was drawn into a colourless slash.

He watched her, wondering if she was still angry over his late night invasion or beset with worry for his grandfather.

He tried to strike up a conversation as he made his breakfast, but Solano answered in single syllables and refused to meet his gaze.

He finally gave up and resigned himself to her silence. He quietly watched her as she finished eating, then rose and set her dishes in the sink.

"I'm going for a walk." She left by the back door, closing it a little too firmly behind her.

Daniel didn't reply. He imagined she'd cool off sooner or later. He swallowed the last bite of toast, then set his own dishes in the sink. He bent to pet Cassandra, who was sleeping in the corner, before leaving the kitchen.

He might as well keep busy, he decided as he mounted the stairs. The den and darkroom were the worst mess of all, so he decided to start there.

He felt overwhelmed as he entered the den. Reams of paper littered the floor, along with a mass of file folders. Even the tall bookshelves lining one wall were bare. Their contents were scattered haphazardly over the floor.

He groaned at the job before him, then rolled up his sleeves with determination. He bent down and began to gather up the scattered papers. He had no intention of trying to return them to their rightful place. His grandfather's filing system was beyond him. Instead, he stacked the papers in neat piles and placed them on the filing cabinet.

His grandfather could rearrange them when he returned. That was *if* he returned. The thought popped unexpectedly into his head. Daniel trembled, scolding himself out loud. "Of course he'll come back."

He bent to retrieve another stack of strewn papers and saw a book lying on the floor. He went rigid. One of the adventure novels his grandfather had written was lying less than a metre away. His grandfather's smiling face on the book jacket was staring up at him.

Daniel picked it up, caressing the smooth shiny cover with his fingertips. He took a step toward the bookshelf and heard a floor board creak beneath his feet. The board shifted under his weight.

"Great house you've got here," he said aloud to the picture of his grandfather. "Needs a little work, though." He carefully stepped over the loose board and placed the book on the shelf.

He bent to examine the board, then caught a glint of silver beneath the desk. He reached out and picked up a small leather bound book with the word *Diary* engraved across its front. *Harold Christie* was etched in the corner in silver ink.

Examining the book, Daniel struggled to make a decision. Should he invade his grandfather's privacy? Would the diary hold any clues that might unravel the mystery surrounding his grandfather's disappearance?

He was filled with doubt, but he stifled it and flipped the book open. Then he began to read the entries inside. He immediately recognized his grandfather's flowing handwriting.

He paused at an entry midway through the book. His throat grew dry. The entry was dated several weeks ago. In flowing script it read:

> Solano arrived today. The hospital stay was obviously a good choice. Her psychiatrist tells us that it could take years before she is back to her former self, though her health seems to have improved greatly. I do sense that she is still a very angry girl. She appears to have difficulty controlling her temper and disappears for hours at a time. We haven't discovered where she goes, but this is of no consequence. She no doubt needs her space after all she has been through. Her part in her father's death still weighs heavily on her mind.

Daniel nearly dropped the book, his hands were shaking so badly. What had his grandfather got himself involved in? What did all of this mean? Why was Solano under psychiatric care? How had she been responsible for her father's death?

Daniel sat down on the floor and flipped back and forth through the pages searching for clues. A clock, hidden somewhere under the jumble of books and paper, slowly ticked off the time as Daniel read each entry. But there were no clues to be found. Only more questions.

There were several accounts that outlined the strange transformation that was taking place on the island. His grandfather had made notes describing the apparent lack of wildlife. He spoke of trees and plants that seemed to be withering and dying. But nothing seemed to explain why death was encroaching on the land.

Daniel discovered a few scattered references about Solano's hospital stay, and a few cryptic notes about fishing trips and jaunts to the other Gulf Islands. But nothing seemed to provide even a clue to the building mystery on Suspicion Island.

The final entry in the book stopped Daniel cold. It was dated the same day that Daniel had received his grandfather's warning phone call. He read the words with growing fear.

I had never imagined that I would stumble upon such a thing when I was investigating the light in the cove. Old Jeb was right after all. Death has come to Suspicion Island.

10.

A thin film of sweat broke out on Daniel's upper lip as he reread the words. Was this the same light that he had seen last night in the cove? He had a sudden mental image of the pale light and the cloaked figure on the beach.

The air inside the room seemed to turn cold.

Daniel was startled when Solano suddenly appeared in the doorway. He had been so engrossed in his grandfather's journal that he had not heard her approach.

"What are you doing?" she asked. All of her previous anger seemed to have disappeared. She looked relaxed as she stood by the desk, staring down at the journal still clutched in Daniel's hand.

"Trying to find out what happened to Grandpa." He looked at her, recalling what his grandfather had written. Could she see mistrust written on his face?

"Did you?"

"Did I what?" His eyebrows furrowed.

"Did you find out what happened to your grandfather?"

"I guess I know more than I did this morning." He motioned to the diary. He was not anxious to tell Solano what he had learned about her past.

He tried to stand, but his legs were filled with pins and needles. He rubbed at his thighs, trying to work out the tension, then groaned as he slowly rose.

He waited until the dull pain subsided, then glanced out the window and saw that the sun was now high in the sky. He had been sitting on the floor in the same position for hours, he realized. It would be well after lunch by now. It seemed hard to believe that less than forty-eight hours had passed since he had arrived on Suspicion Island.

"What's that?" Solano asked, gesturing to the journal.

"It's Grandpa's diary." He sighed. Maybe it was still possible to hide what he knew about her after all.

"And . . . "

He opened the journal to the final entry and read it aloud. As she listened, her skin turned pale.

"I saw a light in the cove lots of times when I first came to live here."

"Did you talk to Grandpa about it?" Daniel asked.

"Yeah," Solano's forehead creased, "but he said it was nothing to worry about. Said it was just a reflection off the moon."

Daniel stared at her dumbstruck. Why would his grandfather have lied about the lights? It was obvious that he had been intrigued with them. Was her state of mind too precarious? Had his grandfather been trying to protect her?

"What are we going to do?" Solano asked.

"I don't know about you," Daniel set the diary on the edge of the desk, "but I'm going to go to the cove. Grandpa must have uncovered something there and if I'm lucky I might too."

"Yeah," Solano said, "but look where it got your grandfather!"

11

Daniel stared out the window of his grandfather's den. He tried not to dwell on his new-found knowledge about Solano. He couldn't make any sense of the sketchy diary entries anyway. There were simply too many unanswered questions.

"Do you think we can climb the point into the cove?" he asked.

"No way. Those rocks are dangerous." Solano ran her finger over the silver lettering on his grandfather's diary and Daniel held his breath. "We'd have to drag the rowboat out of the bush and ride to the cove."

"Well, let's go do it." Daniel started toward the hallway.

"You go ahead and get the boat." Solano followed him into the hall. "I've got some things I have to do."

"Can't it wait?" he asked.

"No." Solano's stance was firm and she didn't look about to change her mind.

"Oh . . . okay . . . " Daniel sputtered. What could Solano have to do that was so important? He hesitated on the first step. He would rather have had Solano with him. At least that way he could keep an eye on her.

He walked downstairs and went outside feeling troubled. What if Solano read the diary? What would she do if she knew he was aware of her secrets? He forced himself not to think about it. Without the boat they didn't have a chance of discovering what was going on in the cove.

Outside, the sun was dimmed by dark clouds. The moisture from the night's rain hung in the air creating an unbearable humidity. And it felt like a storm was brewing. Invisible electricity seemed to be vibrating through the air.

At the bottom of the steps, he glanced toward the trees that hid the pathway to the east side of the island, but decided to follow the beach instead. After reading his grandfather's journal he felt too unnerved to face the silence in the woods.

His jeans and long-sleeved shirt clung damply to him as he skirted the sandy shore.

The scenery circling the island was unremarkable. There was an endless expanse of sand and the blue-green of the water. It was almost impossible to tell how far he had gone, everything looked so much the same.

Ages seemed to pass before he had circled the eastern shoreline and started northward. Within moments he spotted the deep grooves in the sand. They were beginning to disappear near the shore beneath the waves. But his own and Solano's footprints were still visible near the bush.

He followed the ridge into the trees, then paused at the sight of the boat, now fully exposed, a few metres away.

Worry for his grandfather struck him like a fist. His back was set in stiff determination as he walked to the boat and began to drag it out of the trees and onto the beach.

A strong breeze suddenly drove in from the north, whipping his shoulder-length hair into his eyes along with grains of gritty sand. The sun seemed to suddenly wink out as a bank of dark clouds rolled in.

Sweat soaked his clothes from the exertion, then chilled him as the wind swept over the shore. In spite of its size, the boat was heavy and awkward. But Daniel refused to give up. He tugged on it until it finally came to rest at the edge of the water.

After bending down to splash cool water on his face, he took off his running shoes and socks, rolled up his pant legs, then stepped into the ocean. He held the boat steady with one hand, then heaved himself over the side. The small craft rocked for several seconds until he adjusted his weight, then settled down to a gentle roll. He sat down on the wooden seat, facing the stern, then grabbed the oars off their mooring pegs and began to row away from the shore. Each stroke was made more difficult by the rising wind.

When he was several metres from the beach, he turned and steered around the eastern shore of the island. Every few seconds he stole a glance over his shoulder, paying careful attention to the position of the boat. It would be easy to be dragged farther away from the island, and he knew that the boat would be at the mercy of the currents. As he heaved at the oars the lighthouse came into view, reminding him of the hazards of the sea.

His limbs felt revitalized when he finally rounded the south side of the island. The sight of the dock in the distance was a relief. He pulled the oars through the water with renewed vigour.

Before Daniel had secured the boat to the dock, the elements had taken a grip on the island. The wind shrieked through the trees as he tied the boat and started up the staircase to the house. Gnarled limbs reached out, clutching at his arms and legs. A threatening cloud hung like a shroud over the sky.

It was the witching hour, or so it seemed, when he finally entered the living room. The house seemed to sway with the buffeting of the wind, and the overhead lights flickered on and off.

Even Solano appeared not to be herself. She was nestled on the edge of the sofa. Her legs were pulled up beneath her and she was staring sadly out at the storm.

"Bad things happen when the night comes before the day departs." She spoke the words as though reciting some treasured poem from the past. She seemed to be speaking to herself and did not turn to look at Daniel.

He glanced out the window and nodded. Rain was now pelting the glass and the sun was concealed beneath a threatening black sky.

"We'll have to put off our trip to the cove until there's a break in the storm."

"My father died on a day like this." Solano didn't seem to have heard him speak.

Daniel sat down on a big overstuffed chair across from her and studied her face. She seemed so sad . . . so lost. There was something innocent and childlike about the lines of her face. But her eyes looked as though they had seen too much. They were filled with pain unlike any he had seen before.

"You must miss him," Daniel said. He was afraid to break the innocent spell that had captured Solano. The hot-headed girl had disappeared.

"No."

"You're glad he's dead!" Daniel croaked.

"I didn't say that." There was no anger in her reply. She turned and their eyes met. "My father was a cruel man. You can't imagine the horror my mother lived through with him."

"What about you?" Daniel asked. If things were that bad for her mother, some of the nightmare must have fallen on her. Hadn't the diary said that she was responsible for her father's death? What could have prompted such action?

"I loved him once." Solano turned and gazed out the window again, her fingers drawing circles on the brown flesh of her knee.

"What was it like growing up in Montana?" Daniel could sense that the subject of her father was closed, but he wanted to keep her talking. He needed to find some answers to the mystery surrounding her past.

"Life is very different on the reserve. It doesn't matter what kind of house you live in or what you own. You're just accepted as you are."

Solano's voice took on a lilting tone.

"And you never get lonely. There's always someone to talk to . . . someone to hold you when you're sad."

Solano began braiding her long hair as she continued to gaze blindly out the window. Daniel was again reminded of the princess he had imagined earlier. He wanted to reach out to her . . . touch her hair and make all the sadness go away. But he only blushed and kept his hands in his lap.

"And the land is so beautiful," she sighed. "Wildflowers grow everywhere and the scent of sweetgrass hangs in the air like perfume. And there are mountains and rolling plains . . ." She stopped speaking and tied the end of her braid in a little knot.

"It sounds terrific," Daniel smiled. "I guess you must look forward to going back some day."

The wistful look disappeared from Solano's face. A deep frown clouded her features and the light in her eyes died. "I can never go back."

"Why not?" Daniel couldn't understand the finality of her words or the coldness in her voice.

"I'm tired now." Solano stood and walked slowly up the stairs.

Daniel watched her wordlessly, then rested his head back against the chair and tried to sort out the roller coaster of his emotions.

Solano was like fire and ice. One moment she spoke softly, obviously touched by the beauty around her. In the next moment she was filled with anger and pain that darkened the passion in her eyes.

One part of Daniel wanted to gather Solano up protectively like a child. But another stronger part rebelled at the very thought. The diary entries had added fuel to the fire. Her mysterious past served as a sinister backdrop to the questions surrounding his grandfather's disappearance: the disabled two-way radio, the hidden boat, the shadowy figure on the beach, the mysterious disappearing syringe and vial, and the myriad other unexplained bits of the puzzle.

Added to this was the reclusive Jeb Palmer with his claims that the island was dying. And worst of all, Daniel was beginning to think the old man might be right. There seemed to be no life on the island except for a few sea gulls streaking through the sky.

Daniel tried to push the tumult of thoughts away. He was exhausted, though it was only early evening. He was certain that he would not sleep well that night.

The hours slipped by as he let his thoughts drift, conjuring up fiendish plots and hopeless images of his grandfather's fate.

He fell asleep on the sofa as evening gave way to night and the storm raged outside. Solano had still not come down from her room when he finally drifted off to sleep.

12.

The house was quiet when Daniel awoke. He sat up feeling stiff and sore. As the cobwebs of sleep drifted away, he looked at the clock on the wall. He could hardly believe that he had slept so long. It was well after ten o'clock. The sun was shining brightly in the window.

His clothes were wrinkled and he felt hot and damp. Had he dreamed during the night? Some nightmare that refused to be remembered? He grabbed his duffel bag from where he had left it by the door and padded up the stairs past Solano's closed door. Was she still sound asleep? Or was she lying in bed thinking of her home in Montana? He reached out and rapped on the door.

"Hey, Solano, let's get a move on."

"What are you talking about?" Her voice, from the other side of the door, sounded thick with sleep.

"Don't you want to go to the cove with me?"

"Oh . . . yeah . . . sure. Give me a few minutes to get dressed."

"Make it quick!" Daniel continued down the hall to the bathroom. He could hardly wait to get dressed and get to the cove. A new sense of hope prodded at him. Would there be answers to all the mysteries there?

He took a quick shower, brushed his teeth, then changed into a T-shirt and jeans. He walked back down the hall to Solano's room.

"You ready?" He hesitated in the hallway, then reached out and knocked lightly on the door. It swung open a crack.

"Hold your horses," Solano bellowed.

Daniel leaned forward and peered in through the crack, then froze. In the narrow opening he saw Solano sitting on the edge of the bed. She seemed unaware that he was watching her through the crack. She took a guarded look toward the door, then scooped something up from the crumpled blankets beside her. The muscles in Daniel's stomach contracted as he saw a flash of a syringe before Solano dropped it into the drawer of the night stand.

He took a step back and stared in confusion at the grainy surface of Solano's door. Was his imagination playing tricks on him? Had he imagined the objects once more?

He had no time to think about what he had seen. Solano's door flew open and she stepped out into the hall. She had a smile on her face and her faraway look of the night before had disappeared. Her long hair was braided and hung over her left shoulder to her waist. Her eyes were sparkling like two black jewels.

"Well, don't stand there staring. Let's get a move on!"

"Yeah . . . okay." Daniel turned and followed her down the stairs.

He tried not to think of what he had seen. He didn't even want to consider that Solano might be some kind of drug addict. But his doubt wouldn't go away. It would all make so much sense. Maybe that was why she was in such a rush to get back to the house the other day. Maybe she'd needed a fix. Maybe that explained her dazed look the night before.

The more he thought about it, the more sense it seemed to make. Hadn't his grandfather's diary mentioned that Solano disappeared for hours at a time? Maybe she had to sneak away to shoot up away from everyone's prying eyes.

"Earth to Daniel. Earth to Daniel." Solano's taunting voice interrupted his thoughts.

"Huh . . . Were you talking to me?" He paused on the dock next to the boat.

"I said, what do you think we'll find at the cove?"

"I . . . ah . . . I don't know. I guess we'll just have to wait and find out." He stepped into the boat, then gripped the dock to steady it as Solano stepped to the stern and sat facing him.

"You better put this on." Daniel flung one of the life-jackets at her, then grabbed the second one and put it on. There was something comforting about the click of the fastener as it snapped into place.

He pushed the boat away from the dock and grabbed the oars. He tried to concentrate on the heat that pressed into his back instead of the secrets that might be hidden beyond the rocky point, or the secrets that Solano seemed to be concealing beneath her innocent mask.

His jaw was set determinedly as he struggled to row the boat along the island's shore. He slowed as he glanced over his shoulder and recognized the stretch of sand where he had seen Jeb Palmer sitting on the log. The beach was vacant. There was no sign of the old man.

He rowed further along to the rocky promontory jutting out into the ocean.

The rocks ran more than fifteen metres out into the water. They served as a barrier to the cove beyond, isolating it from the rest of the island.

As they neared the point, a strong current began to tug at the boat. It threatened in one moment to pull the boat out into deeper water, then in the next moment tried to heave it against the rocks. He could see Solano tensing, her jaw tight, her eyes flicking nervously over his shoulder. She grasped the sides of the boat with white-knuckled fingers.

He tried to ignore her fear as the boat became harder and harder to handle. He had to fight the mounting current with each passing second, constantly turning his head to ensure that they weren't drawing too near the rocky promontory.

The bow rose into the air, then thudded back down, splashing water over the sides. Daniel nearly tumbled forward into Solano. He gripped the oars to steady himself, then glanced behind him. The waves were once again pushing the craft treacherously close to the rocks.

Daniel bit his upper lip purposefully. The muscles in his arms strained as he fought to keep the boat from being smashed against the waiting rocks. He was so intent upon his task, he was only faintly aware of the foul scent that drifted on the breeze. A smell so putrid that it could not be identified.

"Yuck!" Solano muttered. Her face was pinched with disgust.

He ignored her comment and the smell that seemed to worsen by the second. He fought to steer the boat clear of the rocks. Finally, the ocean seemed to give up its fight. The boat twisted around the point and glided into the smooth water of the cove. It bobbed gently on the waves as Daniel relaxed his arms and shoulders and loosened his fierce grip on the oars.

The sun hovered high in the eastern sky, turning the waves a burnished orange. But despite the glow, Daniel felt a cold chill. A powerful stench filled the air. He turned and looked at the beach. It was littered with dead fish. Some had only recently died, but others were nothing more than a tangle of shiny white bones. Several fish in the final throes of death flapped their weakened bodies along the water's edge. The carcasses of several birds lay amid the scattered bones.

The trees that hugged the towering walls of the cove were withered and grey and bare of leaves. The mossy grass and lichen that grew on the rocky outcrops had turned a rusty brown.

Daniel breathed a muttered curse and swung his legs over the seat. He held a hand over his nose as he faced the beach.

"My, god! What happened here?" Solano's voice was small and weak behind him.

Daniel didn't bother to reply. He had no idea what could have caused such destruction. It appeared as though a horrible disease had swept in and strangled the very life from the cove.

He looked around at the sheer rock out-crops. The cove was completely isolated from the rest of the island. The house on the peak of the hill was barely visible from below. It was nearly hidden by the towering rock face.

The promontories on either side of the cove served as sound barriers. Daniel could barely hear the waves that crashed relentlessly on the other side of the rocks. The silence in the cove was unnerving.

He tried closing his eyes against the gruesome sight on the sand, but it would not be denied. The smell of rotting fish was nearly overpowering.

A sour taste inched its way to his throat, and Daniel's head swam.

Disappointment settled heavily on his shoulders. There were no answers to be dis-covered here among the scattered corpses — just a heap of rotting flesh and bones and yet another question added to the mounting pile.

"Do you think this is what shook Grandpa up so much?" He voiced his thoughts aloud. "I can't believe he never mentioned this to you." He turned around and looked at Solano.

"No one tells me anything!" she said. The corners of her mouth turned down in a pout. "Mom and Harold both treat me like I'm a baby."

Daniel nodded sympathetically, though he wasn't feeling sympathetic at all. Maybe Solano couldn't be trusted to hear any bad news. Maybe no one told her anything because they were afraid that it would send her on a binge of drugs or God knows what.

He turned his head and watched as the sun produced blazing slashes of swirling pinks and oranges across the sky.

"Let's get out of here. It smells disgusting!" Solano begged.

Daniel shifted his body around, then gripped the oars and shoved the boat off the sand. The morning sunlight reflected in the ocean as he began the journey back to the house.

He held his breath as they rounded the point and were immediately sucked into the lashing waters. The foul stench of the cove disappeared on a shifting breeze. He tried to concentrate on the blue sky above as the corpse-strewn beach disappeared behind the grey stone outcrop.

He fought the driving waves until he felt the boat levelling off and the angry water releasing its grasp. The craft escaped into the calm waters along the shore on the other side of the cove.

"I guess we've met our final dead end now." Daniel sighed. "I can't even think of what to do next. I think we've turned over every rock on the island now."

"Except . . . for one." Solano spoke haltingly. He stopped rowing and stared at her.

"What are you talking about?"

"Jeb!" Solano held the side of the boat as their eyes met. "He's the only stone unturned."

"I suppose you're right. He must have some idea what's going on around here. Or at least what's causing everything to die in the cove."

"I guess we'll just have to ask him."

"But I thought you didn't want to go near him."

"I don't!" Solano brushed a wisp of loose hair from her eyes. "But I don't see any way around it. Where else can we turn?"

"I suppose so." Daniel tightened his grip on the oars again and rowed back along the shore.

He fell silent as he steered the boat for the stretch of beach where he had first spoken to Jeb Palmer.

13.

The air was filled with a heavy silence as Daniel rowed the boat to shore, then dragged it up onto the sand. It was a silence that reminded him of their gruesome discovery in the cove. How long would it be before the horrible scourge began to spread to the rest of the landscape? Was it only a matter of time before fish lay withering on every stretch of the sandy shore surrounding the island, before the trees shed their leaves and the spongy moss on the forest floor shriveled in rusty patches?

He tried hard to concentrate on the feel of the sand beneath his runners. He tried to block out the tired ache that seemed to fill his limbs as he surveyed the vacant beach and the thick stand of trees beyond.

"I think he lives down there." Solano stepped to his side and pointed to a narrow footpath that disappeared into the underbrush.

"Let's go see."

They started across the sand and then into the bush.

The trees on either side of the path appeared to have been cleared by a sharp blade. The image of Jeb wielding an axe sent shivers through Daniel. He was filled with second thoughts. Was Solano right to be so afraid of Jeb? Had his grandfather fallen prey to this strange hermit?

He stifled the thoughts as they followed the path that meandered through the trees. They both paused moments later when the path came to an abrupt halt. A small house sat nestled in an open meadow.

It was really no more than a shack. The roof seemed to sag on the left side beneath the weight of a crooked brick chimney. Several panes of glass were missing from two narrow windows on either side of the door. They had been repaired with strips of rotting plywood. The door itself hung open a crack, held on by leather thongs.

The meadow lay in sharp contrast to the tumbledown state of the shack. The grass was freshly trimmed and flowers grew in abundance in neat little borders. A garden sat to the right. The air was filled with the perfumed scent of greenery. It was a slice of paradise nestled in the trees.

The beauty of the scene disappeared as Daniel remembered the reason he had come. He needed to find out if Jeb Palmer was part of the craziness that was taking place on the island.

"Should we just go knock on the door?" Daniel looked at Solano, standing uneasily at his side.

"I guess so . . . you go first though." She gave Daniel a gentle shove.

"Yeah. Sure." Daniel turned and tried to muster up his courage. He started toward the run-down shack.

He took a deep breath as he reached out and rapped on the side of the house. The door looked ready to fall off with the least jarring. He stepped back and waited. Solano stood close behind him. He could feel her warm breath on the back of his neck.

The sunlight seemed to dim as they waited for a reply, but none came.

He was touched by indecision. Should they leave while they still could? But what was the use of running away? There was no comfort to be found in returning to the house on the hill.

"Hello. Anybody home?" Daniel called out, then gave the door a gentle shove. It swung soundlessly open. Still there was no reply. He leaned forward with his hands on the doorjamb and looked inside.

The inside of the little shack was one single room. An area that served as the kitchen held a potbellied stove and a rickety table with one lone chair. A couch separated the kitchen from the living room, if it could be called that. The legs of the sofa were missing. It was held off the grey wooden floor by split logs. Tufts of woolly off-white stuffing stuck out in disarray. A rusty bed frame held a mattress that looked lumpy and uncomfortable beneath a patchwork quilt. Several of the patches were curled up and clung only by a thread.

Despite the shabbiness of the cabin, the walls were covered in paintings so beautiful that they took Daniel's breath away. A fawn, lying in a meadow, had been captured in tiny, precise strokes. A sea-gull screamed out over the raging sea and wildflowers appeared to ripple in an invisible breeze on another canvas. Every wall was covered with the remarkable paintings.

"Will you get a load of this?" Daniel stepped over the threshold. He was immediately surrounded by the smell of oil paint and turpentine.

"Are you crazy?" Solano hissed and tugged on his sleeve.

"Don't worry about it." Daniel took a step further inside. "He's not here." He jerked Solano into the shack beside him.

Solano gasped as she too caught sight of the paintings. "I wonder who did them?" Daniel whispered. He tiptoed across the living room and paused in front of one of the many canvases.

"Are they signed?" Solano asked.

"You won't believe it." Daniel shook his head as he read the name that was scrawled in the right hand corner.

"Well . . . don't keep me in suspense!" Solano sounded annoyed.

"It says 'Jeb Palmer'." Daniel leaned closer for a better look. He could hardly believe his own eyes.

"Whaddaya want?" A man's voice split the silence and Solano let out a frightened yelp.

Daniel spun around and stared in fear and surprise. Jeb stood in the doorway. His large frame blocked out the sunlight.

Solano backed closer to Daniel. She looked like a frightened animal about to bolt.

"I . . . I saw the cove," Daniel sputtered, cursing himself for letting his curiosity get the best of him. The paintings, though beautiful, didn't seem to matter, with Jeb's menacing frame blocking the only doorway out of the shack.

"Did ya, now?" Jeb placed his hands on his hips and stepped closer to Solano. A shaft of light spilled onto the floor behind him. Solano took another step closer to Daniel.

"I found my grandfather's diary. I think he went missing because of what he saw there." Daniel rushed on. His hands began to shake.

"Something bad's going on in the cove," Jeb imparted. "Starting to spread too." He motioned for Daniel and Solano to follow him outside. Solano threw Daniel a scathing I-told-you-so look before following Jeb outside.

Daniel stepped into the clear morning sunshine with a sense of relief. He drew in deep gulps of fresh air as Jeb continued out past the garden toward the hill at the back of the shack.

"It's starting to spread." Jeb motioned to several withered trees growing on the leading edge of the rocky point. "Cove's just on the other side of that."

"Don't you know what's causing it?" Solano sounded shaky.

"Nope. Heard some strange sounds coming from there a few nights back. See some odd lights every once in a while too. Don't think I wanna know either."

Jeb bent down and picked up a hoe that lay on the ground nearby. Daniel and Solano stepped back two paces. Jeb smiled.

"Why not?" asked Daniel. The sight of Jeb holding the weapon in his hands caused his voice to crackle.

"Look where it got your grandaddy!"

Daniel nodded and breathed a sigh of relief as Jeb let the hoe drop back to the ground.

"You get your phone working yet?" the old man asked.

"Nope." Daniel held his ground. "Someone destroyed the two-way in the lighthouse, too." He glanced at Solano and saw her lips close down in a tight line. He turned back and saw that Jeb actually looked startled at the revelation.

For the first time, Daniel saw genuine concern spread over Jeb's face. "Seems we got ourselves a regular mystery here, now don't we?" The old man ran a big hand through his hair. It was not tied in a ponytail as it had been the day before. It now hung lank across his shoulders.

"Seems so." Daniel nodded. "Looks as though someone doesn't want us to get hold of the police either."

"You wouldn't be pointing fingers, now would ya?" Jeb asked.

Solano threw Daniel a warning glance, but he ignored it.

"I don't know what to think." Daniel looked accusingly at Solano, then Jeb.

"Well, you're pointing it in the wrong direction. I don't know squat about what's going on in the cove or what happened to your grandaddy."

"That so!" Daniel blurted out. Solano's head spun around and she glared at him. Her eyes were saying, "Are you nuts?"

Jeb's eyebrows rose. He took a step back, looked seriously at Daniel, then flung his head back and laughed — a booming laugh that lit his face with colour. For a moment he looked less frightening — even jovial. Daniel couldn't help but smile.

"You got a lot of guts, kid!" Jeb took a step towards Daniel and put his arm on his shoulder. His eyes sparkled with delight. Solano let out a sigh of relief.

"Don't you worry about your grandaddy. He's a tough old coot. From what I can understand, he's got a way of getting himself out of scrapes." Jeb gave Daniel an almost affectionate slap on the back. It was affectionate, but so hard that it nearly took his breath away. "I wish I could help, but there's really nothing I can do. If the phones ain't working, then there ain't no way off the island till Friday."

"So we're just gonna have to wait it out?" Daniel asked.

"'Fraid so." Jeb turned and started back toward the shack.

"Were you out in the cove the other night?" Daniel asked, suddenly recalling the shrouded figure he had seen. If it wasn't Solano, then it had to be Jeb. There was no one else on the island.

"Nope. I ain't been there for more than a month. Got me a big leak in my boat." He pointed to a small aluminum boat that was leaning against the back of the shack. The bow was twisted and a hole was punctured in its side.

Daniel felt a strange stirring in the pit of his stomach. Jeb was telling the truth.

"Those are really incredible paintings you did," Solano commented. The quaver had disappeared from her voice.

Jeb shrugged as he turned around to face them.

"Painting's what brought me here to Suspicion Island in the first place. Had high ideals way back then." Jeb ran his hand through his hair and looked up at the sky. "Thought I'd just spend a few years doing what I loved best. Never cared much for people anyway."

"How come you never left?" Daniel asked.

"It ain't so easy to leave Paradise once you find it."

Solano nodded her head in agreement. Was she thinking of her life in Montana? Daniel wondered.

Paradise Lost, he thought as he looked up at the perishing trees on the crest of the point.

"If you're afraid, you're welcome to stay here with me," Jeb offered. He glanced from Solano to Daniel.

Daniel stood staring back at Jeb in surprise. The offer was so unexpected that he felt a lump grow in his throat.

"Nah, we'll . . . be fine," Daniel sputtered, not wanting Jeb and Solano to see how frightened he really was — afraid to return to the silence of his grandfather's house, afraid of the loneliness that was creeping slowly into him, afraid that he'd never see his grandfather again.

"Well, if you change your mind, you know where to find me." Jeb disappeared into the house.

14.

Daniel and Solano spent the rest of the day combing the island for clues. By late afternoon they had covered the island on foot, checking out every conceivable cranny for some key to the unexplained. As afternoon turned to evening they got back in the rowboat and circled the island, returning once more to the cove. But they found nothing — not even one clue to help shed light on the puzzle looming over Suspicion Island.

It was dark when they finally returned to the house, dragging their feet.

Daniel tried to ignore the heavy silence that surrounded him as he scooped Cassandra off the floor and brushed his hand over her glistening fur.

"I think I'm going to go lie down. I'm wiped out," he said as he started up the staircase to the second floor.

"I'm just gonna grab something to eat, then I think I'll go lie down too. I feel like crap!"

"Yeah, you'd don't look so hot." Daniel glanced at her over the railing. Solano's face was pale and her eyes looked hooded and dark. "Maybe you just need some nourishment," he commented, then nearly laughed with the irony of it all. Maybe the nourishment Solano needed didn't come in the form of a sandwich and a glass of milk. Maybe what she needed came in the end of needle and a milky white vial!

"Catch you later." He forced the frightening thought away, still holding Cassandra. He set the old cat on the bed and stripped off his clothes. He lay down on the mattress, pulled a blanket over himself, then lay back to listen to Cassandra's muted purrs.

With his head turned toward the window, he watched as a fluffy cloud drifted through the dark sky. Finally he fell into a fitful sleep.

He awoke hours later surrounded by night. Bits and pieces of a lingering dream hovered in his mind: his grandfather's smiling face, Solano sitting on a hill, her long dark hair lifting in an invisible breeze around her shoulders.

Before he could shake free of sleep, he imagined that he was at home in his own bed. He glanced across the room, wondering if his parents were asleep in the next room. Disappointment filled him as he came fully awake and saw the antique bedpost at the foot of the bed and the battered dresser in the shadowy light. He was in his grandfather's house on Suspicion Island, he reminded himself with a heavy heart.

He pinched his eyes closed once more, but sleep evaded him. The horrible reality of his situation returned with sudden clarity.

Slowly he rose and walked to the window, looking down at the waters that surrounded the island. A howling wind had arisen during the night. The trees next to the house bent under its force, and the water below was capped by white frothing foam.

Daniel went numb as a flicker of movement in the distance caught his eye.

Once again there was someone on the beach in the cove. He squinted his eyes, certain that he was only seeing a flash of memory from the previous night. But when he reopened them, the figure was still on the beach. A pale beam of light illuminated the sand.

Who was walking in the secluded cove?

Turning, he quickly grabbed his jeans and sweatshirt from the heap on the floor and pulled them on. He stepped into his running shoes, not even bothering to tie the laces. He raced out of the bedroom and stood in front of Solano's door. Would she be fast asleep on the other side? Or was she down in the cove?

He flung the door open, certain that her bed would be empty. Relief and surprise flooded him as he saw an unmoving lump in the middle of the bed.

"Who's there?" Solano suddenly bolted upright. She thrust her hands before her as if to ward off an attack. The moonlight caught her hair cascading around her shoulders.

"It's me, Daniel." He reached out and flicked on her bedroom light. Solano immediately shielded her eyes against the glare. "There's someone in the cove. I'm going to see who it is."

"Give me a minute to get dressed. I'll come with you." Solano swung her legs over the bed sleepily, then gave her head a shake.

"I'll meet you down on the dock." Daniel turned and rushed down the dark staircase. Cassandra gave a mew of protest as he sailed down the stairs.

Daniel sped out into the night.

The boat was banging noisily against the dock when Daniel arrived at the beach. Though the night sky overhead was cloudless, a strong wind was rolling off the ocean, sending a blast through his hair.

He shivered as he squatted down and untied the short length of rope that secured the boat. He stepped in, then waited anxious moments until Solano came streaking down the stairs and across the beach, hair flying up behind her. Her feet made an odd hollow thud on the dock.

"I'm scared, Daniel," Solano admitted after she stepped into the boat and sat down facing him.

"Me too." Daniel said the words quietly, hoping she wouldn't hear.

The muscles in his arms strained as he grabbed the oars and started toward the cove.

The wind pushed fiercely at the small craft. For every stroke that he propelled them forward, the driving force of the wind seemed to push them back two. He tightened his grasp on the wooden oars and pulled them through the water with long, even strokes.

The path that led to Jeb's shack looked dark and deserted as they passed and continued westward.

Sweat trickled down Daniel's back, but finally they began to make headway. They were quickly nearing the treacherous water off the cove.

"This might have been a bad idea," Solano said the moment they entered the churning water near the rocks. The boat was suddenly spun around so that it was facing the way they had come. In an instant the boat was trapped on the crest of a huge wave. The wave receded in a rush and they dropped back down with a jarring thud. A flood of water rushed in, immediately soaking them.

"Watch out!" Daniel yelled a warning as a second swell came from beneath the boat, sending the bow out of the ocean and up into the air. The boat hovered perilously on the crest of the wave. One oar snapped against the rocks and shattered like glass. The vibration shot up Daniel's arm like rocket fire as splinters flew into the sky, then returned to the boiling sea and immediately disappeared.

The wave suddenly receded, and for several seconds the boat righted itself. Then another wave smashed into the bow.

Daniel dropped the second oar and grabbed the sides of the boat with white-knuckled fingers as the small craft was heaved like a rag doll toward the point. He saw horror slip over Solano's face and tried to shout a warning to her as the boat careened towards the rocks. But his words were drowned out by her strangled scream as she snapped her head backwards to face the cove.

A scream that echoed Solano's tore from Daniel's own throat as the point suddenly hovered in front of them. He sailed into the air as the stern hit the rocks. He saw a flash of black hair as he sailed over Solano's head. Before the icy water closed over him, he caught sight of the two life-jackets bobbing out of reach on the dark waves.

Daniel's eyes stung and salty water flowed freely into his mouth and nose as the ocean overtook him. The raging water was sucking him down, farther and farther. In an instant he knew that he was going to die.

"Don't give up." The words sounded a million miles away. The voice was strangely not his own, but rather, the booming tone of his grandfather. "Keep fighting!"

Daniel began to struggle against the ocean that was overtaking him.

His lungs felt ready to explode as his head finally burst out of the water. He looked around. Where was Solano? He couldn't see her in the frothing water. Everything was black and swirling before him. Then suddenly her arm burst out of the water less than a metre away. Her fingers were limp and lifeless. Daniel dove across the distance and gripped her wrist in a steely grasp. Was she alive?

The water once again started to drag him down and he began to kick his feet. He looked frantically around for some safe harbour. He didn't even pause to think as he caught sight of the rocks nearby. He dragged Solano's limp body toward the rocky outcrop.

He struggled for a grip and, with the last of his energy, pulled himself up onto the slippery rocks. He dragged Solano out behind him.

His running shoes had been torn from his feet in the surging ocean. His bare feet had little traction on the slick ledge, but Daniel refused to give up. He continued to scramble up the slippery outcrop, dragging Solano until he was far out of reach of the lashing waves.

He lay back on the rocks for several moments. He was chilled to the bone and his limbs refused to move. Slowly, he regained his strength and looked down at Solano. The moonlight was shining down on her still form. Her face was expressionless, her hair like seaweed around her. Her chest didn't appear to be moving.

"Solano . . . Solano. Don't die. Please . . . " He reached out and ran his hand uselessly over her smooth forehead. Ignoring the sharp searing pain, he shoved his feet between the rocks and tried to draw Solano to a sitting position. Her body was limp in his arms.

He slapped her firmly on the back and water immediately spilled from her lips. He repeated the procedure, her chest heaved, and a fountain of water sprang from her mouth.

Happiness flooded Daniel as her eyes flew open and their eyes met.

"Are you all right?" Daniel asked.

"I thought I was going to die," Solano said, hacking. She leaned hard into Daniel's chest. He held her firmly in his arms until the coughing subsided.

"You're not the only one!" Daniel felt himself slipping on the glistening rocks. He let go of Solano and fought for a foothold. He jammed his bare feet between two grey stones and pressed down with his knees. He felt himself slow, then stop.

He scampered back to the crest of the rocks where Solano still sat. She looked frightened. Her hair hung limp around her face. Her eyes were two huge round circles.

"How are we gonna get off here?" Solano asked. She looked down at the churning water below, then turned on her stomach and peered over the rocks. She gasped.

"What's wrong?" Daniel pushed himself upward as a flash of light caught his attention. A beam of light was shining over the crest of the point from the cove on the other side.

Solano dropped her voice to a mere whisper as she spoke. "Someone's in the cove." She tucked her head down, then motioned for Daniel to look over.

He was immediately aware of the rising smell of rotting flesh as he peered over. A lone figure stood on the beach a few metres below.

Daniel ducked out of sight, then lay stock still listening to his own and Solano's breathing. Something jabbed into his flesh as he flattened himself against the rocks.

"Who is it?" Solano breathed.

Daniel shrugged and pushed himself upward again.

From their vantage above, Daniel could watch the shadowy figure. A flashlight was held in the figure's hand. It lit the cove in an unearthly glow.

"You recognize him?" Daniel whispered. He looked at Solano, whose face was screwed into a grimace from the putrid smell drifting toward them. Solano again shook her head.

They both gasped as a gust of wind blew the hood of the figure's rain slicker back. Tangled white hair and a craggy face became visible in the dim light.

"Captain Morrison!" Solano breathed.

Daniel nodded. Even from this distance he could make out the weathered face of the owner of the supply-boat company.

Solano motioned out towards the water and Daniel turned his head. What seemed to be a large tugboat was moored less than a hundred meters from shore. It looked like all the other tugboats that Daniel had ever seen, except that it had been modified. The flat stern deck held a large metal tank. It reminded Daniel of the heavy grey tanks that dotted the prairie oilfields back home.

A thick hose was strung from the tank to the sand, and a smaller inflatable boat was pulled up on shore.

Hidden in the shadows on the point, Daniel watched as Captain Morrison walked across the sand to the inflatable, got in, and began to row towards the tug.

Daniel and Solano slid back into the shadows when Morrison's voice broke the silence of the night.

"Let 'er rip!" His arm swept through the air. The gesture was followed by the sound of a motor spinning to life. Instantly, the hose began to jump across the beach and a foul-smelling brew spilled from its end.

"My God!" Daniel gasped as a dark liquid gurgled onto the sand, splattering the dead fish and piles of bones. "They're dumping some kind of toxic waste." His voice dropped to a murmur. "The island is being poisoned."

"And what about the ocean?" Solano muttered angrily. "How much of that crap is going back into the sea?"

Daniel didn't bother to reply. The answer was obvious in the corpses that littered the sand.

15.

Daniel shifted his body further into the shadows and motioned for Solano to do the same.

"What are we going to do?" Daniel asked.

"Do you think this is what Harold discovered here?"

He nodded. "And I think Morrison's responsible for his disappearance too."

"So what now? We still don't have any way off this island to get help."

"We do now!" Daniel gestured to the tugboat.

"What are you talking about? You're not thinking of trying to get aboard that, are you?"

"Can you think of a better way?" Daniel asked.

"No . . . but . . . what are you going to do? Throw yourself on their mercy and hope they'll take you to the cops so you can report them?"

"Not likely." Daniel rolled his eyes. "But they are my ticket out of here. I don't care if I have to hang on the side of that boat by my teeth. I'm getting off Suspicion Island."

"What's with all this 'I' crap? You're not leaving me here by myself."

"Then you better get ready to do some swimming." Daniel motioned for Solano to follow him over the top of the point.

They crouched in the shadows as Morrison's inflatable boat pulled up next to the tug. They watched as he gripped a ladder on the side of the boat and climbed to the deck. The old man secured the small craft to a series of pulleys and heaved it up. The sound of chains rattled and clanked until the in-flatable boat sat on the tugboat's wheelhouse.

Daniel shifted around and peered back at the hose that was still resting on the sand. Every few seconds the hose gave a jerk and a gurgle, and more of the dark liquid shot onto the thirsty sand. It seemed forever before the gushing liquid trickled to a stop.

"Pull 'er in," Morrison commanded. A second man who detached himself from the shadows near the bow started to pull the hose on board. It made a hollow clugging sound as it dipped into the water, then onto the tug.

"Let's go," Daniel commanded as both Morrison and the second man walked to the front of the boat. Within seconds a powerful engine roared to life.

Daniel stood up and scrambled down the other side of the point. Solano followed close behind. The rocks on the other side were damp, but they lacked the slick glossy finish. The sandy cove protected it from the worst of the sea's splashing.

Daniel nearly stumbled and fell a few times and his feet screamed in agony, but he refused to give up. He leaped the last metre to the sand. He turned back and watched as Solano jumped as well. She sprawled with a thump on the sand beside him.

"What now?" Solano asked as she rose to her feet. She still looked weak and unsteady from their earlier accident. She cast a frightened look at the boat.

"Are you sure you're up for this?" Daniel looked at her doubtfully.

Solano's skin was tinged with an unhealthy colour.

"Don't worry about me." A fiery look returned to her eyes. "I don't need a keeper!"

"Okay . . . okay," Daniel muttered. He shook his head in defeat and admiration. He'd never met anyone as determined as Solano. Most people would probably still be lying on the rocky point trying to catch their breath. Solano was the most stubborn person he'd ever met.

He turned back to face the tug. "I guess our only choice is to swim to the left side of the boat. We should be able to hang onto the ladder until it's safe to go aboard." He stripped off his wet bulky sweatshirt and dropped it on the sand.

Daniel took one final look at the two men on the tug's deck. They were still intently preparing the boat to leave. Morrison stood in the wheelhouse, while the other man operated a winch that lifted the anchor. When this task was done, he joined Morrison in the wheelhouse.

"This is insane," Solano breathed as they both started toward the ocean. They dived into the water and began to swim to the boat.

When they were about twenty-five metres from shore, Daniel felt the shallowness of the water suddenly drop off beneath him. The water grew cold. He instantly understood why the tug hadn't been pulled onto the cove shore. The water was simply too shallow near the beach.

Daniel and Solano cut through the water like a pair of dolphins. And though Daniel's strokes were stronger, Solano had little trouble keeping up. Her swimming technique was obviously well practiced. Her arms cut easily through the waves.

When Daniel reached the side of the craft he gripped the ladder, then reached out and took hold of Solano's wrist. She got a grip on one metal rung and pulled herself up as well. They both clung to the ladder as the boat suddenly began to move forward.

"Made it," Daniel said as he fought to catch his breath. He tried to ignore Solano's worrisome colour. She still looked green around the edges.

He motioned for her to follow him as he drew himself slowly upwards. He got a grip on the edge of the boat and peered over, then went rigid. Morrison and the second man were standing facing seaward in the small covered wheelhouse. The thought of being discovered sent his heart racing. He waited silently, making certain that neither of the men was about to turn around.

Moments passed before he hauled himself over the side of the boat, knowing he could be discovered at any moment. He turned around and helped Solano aboard. He motioned her to follow him as he got down on his stomach and began to slither across the deck. Their wet clothes made a sloshing sound as they crawled along.

They both paused again when they were hidden behind the boat's heavy steel bulkhead and the large metal tank.

Daniel leaned against the cold metal, then let his eyes scan the shadowy deck for a hiding spot.

"Over there," Solano whispered close to his ears. She pointed to a large tarp that lay in a heap nearby.

Daniel nodded, a half-smile creasing his mouth. He crept toward the back of the wheelhouse, then past it to the heap of canvas. He could hear Solano's sloppy clothes on the deck. Would the Captain hear it as well?

When he reached the tarp he lifted up one heavy edge and waited for Solano to slide beneath it. When she was completely covered, he slid in beside her and let the oily tarp drop over them. He was instantly surrounded by the shifting smell of oil and diesel fuel. He covered his nose with the palm of his hand. Tears streaked down his cheeks.

"I don't think I can stand this . . . " Solano whispered, then fell silent. The irregular beat of footfalls shook the deck. Daniel lay perfectly still beside her, praying that she wouldn't speak or cough, and willing himself to do the same. He tried to keep his body from shivering against his cold, wet clothes. The whispering of shoes seemed only inches from his face.

Time seemed to slow to a crawl as they lay like two spoons beneath the oil-soaked tarp. Their bodies were pressed close together. They were both motionless, except for the rapid rise and fall of their chests.

Finally, the footsteps ceased. Daniel heard Solano let out a long sigh, and he heaved one as well.

It seemed as though hours passed as the boat rocked against the waves. Daniel's stomach rolled against the assault.

After what seemed like a lifetime, the constant purr of the engine died and the boat slowed to a stop. Suddenly the air was filled with sounds of activity. Morrison's voice broke the stillness of the night.

"One more run and we're out of here." He sounded jovial. "We'll take care of the hostages tomorrow night after we dump the last load. Then we'll head for the open sea."

"Hostages," Solano breathed. Daniel reached out gently and covered her mouth with his hand. He was rewarded with a sharp jab to the ribs. He dropped his arm and lay still. Solano hadn't lost any of her hellfire despite her fear.

"Where are we movin' the operation to?" an unrecognizable voice asked.

"You'll know when you need to." Morrison replied. The humour had disappeared from his voice. "Now get this boat secured. And don't forget to make sure the hostages are secured for the night. We can't risk those two getting away now."

"Sure thing, Cap. I'll check 'em as soon as I'm done here." The boat vibrated under the heavy tread of feet, then there was silence.

Daniel lay perfectly still. He was not yet certain that he and Solano were alone on the deck.

He waited anxious moments until the air grew quiet. And despite the fact that he was beginning to feel woozy from the stench that surrounded him, he didn't move until he could hear only muffled voices that seemed far away in the distance.

He lifted the edge of the tarp and peered out. Nothing moved. The boat was dark. Even the shadows were strangely still.

"I think they're gone," Daniel whispered.

"Are you sure?" Solano sounded uneasy.

"Not really," Daniel admitted. "But there's only one way to find out." He held his breath and swept the tarp away from them. They both gasped for the first breath of fresh air in what seemed a lifetime.

Daniel sat up and looked out into the night. He got to his knees and half walked, half crawled to the side of the craft. Solano followed him.

Daniel looked overboard, then ducked down as he saw Captain Morrison walking on an unfamiliar beach with another man. Was this the man in charge of securing the hostages? Daniel wondered. Excitement leapt into his throat at the thought of it. Maybe his grandfather was nearby . . . somewhere on this strange island.

Daniel and Solano peered over more cautiously again. The men had turned and were retreating down a path in the trees. The vegetation was less dense on this island. Daniel could see a sprinkling of decrepit-looking buildings amid the trees.

Morrison continued down the path, but the other man veered toward a unpainted shack about a hundred metres from shore.

Daniel watched as he jiggled a heavy dead-bolt on the narrow doorway. Then, appearing satisfied that the door was secure, he too wandered away down the path in the trees.

"Do you think Harold is in there?" Solano asked. There was a catch of excitement in her voice.

"Let's go find out!"

Daniel stood up and scurried down the ladder to the dock below. Solano rushed down behind him. The dock was long and the water looked treacherously deep around it.

They both rushed down it, trying to keep their footfalls quiet in the silence of the night. They raced across the beach to the small building. All thoughts of being caught were forgotten as Daniel slid the dead-bolt back and threw open the door.

Harold Christie looked up from where he lay sprawled on the dirt floor as Daniel and Solano rushed into the room. A dim bulb overhead illuminated his arched eyebrows and open mouth.

Movement in the corner of the room drew Daniel's attention and his head snapped towards it. He was astonished as he came face to face with a woman who looked amazingly like Solano. She had the same glittering black eyes, the same high cheekbones and tawny complexion. Even her hair was as coal-black as Solano's. Her left cheek was swollen and bruised.

"Grandpa." Daniel turned away and flew to his grandfather's side. He hugged him in an excited embrace. Relief made him feel weak and shaky.

"Mom?" Solano stood in the middle of the room and stared at the woman in amazement. "How in the world did you get caught up in this?"

"It's a long story, Solly. Maybe we ought to discuss it later." She rolled onto her side and gestured pleadingly to her wrists. They were bound by thick rope and surrounded by angry red welts.

"What in God's name are you doing here, Danny boy?" His grandfather asked. "I thought I told you not to come."

"Life's full of little surprises, isn't it?" Daniel released his grandfather from his bear hug and motioned over his shoulder to Solano.

His grandfather's face turned red. "I meant to tell you about her. I just thought I'd give your mom some time to adjust to the marriage first."

"Fat chance," Daniel laughed. He could already imagine his mother's face when she discovered that she now had a sixteen-year-old half-sister!

His grandfather looked like a little boy who'd just been caught eating candy before supper. Daniel couldn't help but smile.

The smile faded as he realized that, like Maria, his grandfather's arms were bound behind his back. He flinched as he saw dried blood on the thick rope as he untied the constricting knots.

Daniel swallowed his rising questions about Maria. Wasn't she supposed to be in Vancouver on a photo shoot? How had she ended up as Morrison's captive as well?

"We'll have to finish this reunion another time," Daniel smiled at his grandfather, then turned back to the door. "There's no time to talk. We've got to get out of here. They could come back any moment." Daniel edged toward the door and motioned for the others to follow.

The beach out front was still deserted. He waved the group on. They all ran behind him across the beach to the dock.

"Can you drive this thing?" he asked in a hushed whisper, looking anxiously at his grandfather.

The old man smiled with an adventurous glint in his eyes. It was the look Daniel had seen a hundred times before. "I'll give it my best shot."

"Then go." Daniel helped his grandfather up the short ladder, then followed Solano and her mother aboard.

He was thrown to the floor as his grandfather brought the motor to life and shifted it into reverse. He twisted the wheel to the right, then sharply to the left. The boat shuddered, then pulled away from the dock.

Shouts suddenly filled the air and several men ran across the beach toward them.

Daniel rose to his feet in time to see Captain Morrison take a valiant leap off the dock to the side of the boat. He clung to the lip of the tug for several seconds before plunging into the chilly depths of the ocean.

Daniel gave a howl of delight and embraced Solano in an enthusiastic hug as the boat lumbered away from the island.

16.

Daniel smiled at his grandfather sitting across from him in the living room of the house on Suspicion Island. Maria sat next to him and Cassandra was curled up on his lap.

Daniel had to admit that his grandfather and Maria seemed to share a very special relationship, despite the difference in their ages. They were constantly holding hands or smiling at each other. And Daniel was surprised to admit that he liked Maria too. She was a lot like Solano — full of spunk and energy. But where Solano was quick to anger, Maria was quiet and easy-going.

Daniel turned to Solano and gave her a broad smile. The excitement of their getaway the night before was still rippling through him. Solano smiled back, then turned her attention to the police officer.

"Now, Mr. Christie, let's start at the top. How did you discover that your island was being used as a toxic waste dump?"

"It started when I first noticed these strange lights in the cove. When I first moved here it was only once or twice a week. Then as time went on it got more and more regular."

Maria chimed in. "We went to see Jeb Palmer about it. But he was just as confused as we were. And then he showed us what was happening to the plants and wildlife. It seemed like the whole place was dying off," she added.

"So one night we just started to put two and two together. We decided to find out about those lights. Maria took her camera along and we got some real dandy shots of the whole operation," Harold Christie said.

Maria looked sheepishly at the officer as she spoke up. "I guess a lot of this craziness could have been avoided if I'd kept my big mouth shut." She looked at Daniel's grandfather and smiled weakly. He gave her a reassuring pat on the back.

"Oh, don't blame yourself. It's not like you knew Morrison was involved. After all, he wasn't in on that late-night raid."

"I suppose so." Maria nodded, then continued. "Anyway . . . I thought Morrison might recognize some of the people in the photographs. Him being local and all. Of course he did. Took one look at the pictures, then whacked me on the side of the head." She rubbed her bruised cheek as though remembering the blow.

"The next thing I know, Harold's tied up on the boat beside me, and Morrison's off on the island 'takin' care of business' — whatever that means! I guess he went to look for the photo's negatives."

"That must have been when he destroyed the two-way radio . . . " Daniel broke in and saw his grandfather's surprise.

"And hid Harold's boat in the bush," Solano added.

"Probably wanted you two to think Mr. Christie left the island under his own steam," the police officer suggested.

"Actually, that must have been for Solano's benefit," his grandfather spoke up. "Daniel wasn't supposed to be here!"

"What do you mean?" Solano asked.

"I phoned Daniel as soon as I got back from the cove the night we discovered what was going on. I warned him to stay away from the place."

"Oh sure, you warn him, but you didn't bother to let me know what's going on!" Solano threw Harold and then her mother a scolding look.

"Well . . . ah . . . " Daniel's grandfather stammered.

"We just didn't want to upset you." Maria cut in, looking embarrassed. "You know how much we worry about you."

"Too much, if you ask me." Solano said angrily, then let the subject drop.

"So . . . " the officer cut in and looked at Daniel. "Was it the lights in the cove that tipped you off that there was something strange going on?"

"For the most part," Daniel replied. "I guess it must have been Morrison who was responsible for the lights all along."

"It would seem so." The police officer rose from his chair. "Well, I think that's all I need right now." He placed his cap back on his head and walked to the door. "You realize, of course, that you'll have to leave the island." He turned, lifted his hat, and straightened his short hair. "This place isn't going to be safe to live on for years . . . if ever."

Daniel's grandfather nodded his head sadly.

"I'll let Jeb Palmer know if you like," the officer said.

"He's not going to take the news well." Daniel swallowed hard. He recalled Jeb saying it was hard to leave "Paradise." But Jeb's little piece of paradise had been destroyed! Daniel was glad that he wasn't going to have to be the bearer of bad news.

"So . . . you've met Jeb?" his grandfather asked when the policeman had taken his leave.

"Yeah, he seems like a pretty decent guy." Daniel tried to keep his voice even. Where would the old man go now that his home had been destroyed?

"Look, if you don't mind I'd like to get some air." Daniel suddenly felt as though the walls were pushing in around him. The room seemed to grow smaller and smaller with each passing second.

"Want me to come along?" His grandfather looked concerned.

"Nah," Daniel smiled reassuringly. "I'll be fine. Besides, you and Maria look like you could use a rest." He shifted his eyes to his shoes, surprised by his own words. It suddenly didn't seem so important to have his grandfather all to himself. Was it possible that there was room for all of them in his grandfather's life?

"Yeah, you're probably right." His grandfather dropped down onto the sofa and smiled at Daniel.

"You want to come for a walk?" Daniel turned his attention to Solano. There was still so much he didn't know about her. And he didn't think he'd ever feel totally comfortable around her until he got some answers. Maybe even then! Was she a drug addict? Was she responsible for her own father's death? Maybe he was better off not knowing the truth!

"I guess so." Solano looked at her mother.

"Sure, you two go ahead. Get some air." Maria smiled. "But don't forget to take your needle first, Solly."

"Needle?" Daniel's gasped.

"I'm diabetic." Solano dropped her gaze to the floor. Daniel blanched, feeling the colour draining from his face.

"What's the matter?" Harold jumped up and came to Daniel's side. "You look like you just saw the bogeyman. You're as white as a sheet."

"I'm fine." Daniel laughed. "I guess I did see the bogeyman." Or at least one he'd created on his own. He recalled the image of the syringe and the vial he had seen on Solano's night stand. He remembered Solano's mysterious sickness that seemed to appear and disappear without reason.

"He's got a habit of creating bogeymen." Solano winked at Daniel and burst out laughing.

"Inside joke?" Maria asked, then rolled her eyes when neither Daniel nor Solano tried to explain the remark.

Daniel shook his head and gave a short laugh as Solano rushed up the stairs, then returned moments later.

They both raced for the door at the same time. Daniel stood aside and motioned gallantly for Solano to pass, but she refused.

"You go first. I'm not an invalid."

"Fine," Daniel rolled his eyes in mock disgust at his grandfather and Maria. "Cantankerous as ever!" He breathed.

"I heard that." Solano shoved him into the verandah. He attempted to wave to his grandfather and Maria as she herded him down the steps.

"How come you didn't tell me you were diabetic?" Daniel asked as Solano fell into step beside him.

"Why? So you could treat me like an invalid too? Besides . . . Mom and Harold have that covered." She grabbed Daniel by the sleeve. "Quit dawdling," she scolded.

"You'd think you'd treat me better since I saved your life and all," Daniel said.

"I didn't even come close to drowning," Solano said firmly.

"No, and I suppose you swallowed all that water on purpose!"

"Of course. It's an old native remedy for upset stomach. Sea water that is . . . "

"You're full of it!" Daniel groaned.

They fell silent as they walked down the steps. Daniel was once again struck by the unnatural silence that surrounded them. Was Solano thinking the same thing?

"Don't you find it hard to believe that someone can care so little for the land?" Daniel asked.

"A Salish chief once told me an old Cree prophecy. I didn't realize how true it was until now," Solano said.

"What's the prophecy say?" Daniel asked.

Solano's voice was like a song as she recited the remembered words: "Only after the last tree has been cut down, only after the last river has been poisoned, only after the last fish has been caught, only then will you find that money cannot be eaten."

As she fell silent a faraway look came over her. It was the same look of sadness and pain that she'd had when she'd talked about Montana.

"That's beautiful," Daniel said softly. "I guess you must miss your people and your home in Montana?"

"I can never go back there." Solano looked at Daniel and their eyes locked. "My father's family lives there. They blame me for my dad's death." Her voice cracked.

"Why?"

"It's a long story." She slowed her steps and looked out across the expanse of sand.

"I got nothing but time."

Solano nodded, then shrugged with a look of defeat.

"They think that my decision to run away from home is what killed my father. But I just couldn't take any more of my dad's abuse."

"What happened?" Daniel asked.

They reached the beach and fell into step beside each other.

"Dad could be so great when he wasn't drinking. But once he had a few belts he'd turn into a crazy man. He'd come home and beat the hell out of me and Mom."

As she spoke, Daniel recalled the photograph in Solano's jewelry box. Was it her father's face that had been cut from the photo?

"Anyway, one night he came home drunk and in a rage. Mom was away on a photo shoot. Dad yanked me right out of bed and just started whaling on me." Tears formed in Solano's eyes and she swiped at them angrily. "I waited till he'd fallen asleep and then I just packed my bags and left. I guess I must have woken him up 'cause I hadn't even reached the road before he came out of the house after me. He was madder than I've ever seen him."

"What did you do then?" Daniel prompted her to go on.

"I hid in the bushes. I was hoping he'd finally pass out or just give up if he thought I was gone for good. But that didn't happen." Solano stopped speaking and stared out at the water. "I heard his truck start up and then he drove right past where I was hiding, fishtailing all over the place."

It appeared that Solano was reliving the nightmare again as she spoke. Her arms were crossed over her chest and she was rocking gently back and forth.

"He started smashing into the bushes at the edge of the road. I guess he must have caught a skiff of gravel, 'cause the truck just flipped over into this really steep ditch. There was this horrible sound of twisting metal and then the sky just lit up with flames." Her voice had grown low and tears streamed down her cheeks. "I tried to get him out, I really did." Her voice rose to a fever pitch. "But I couldn't. It was just . . . too hot . . . "

The island around them was still as Solano stopped speaking. She gripped her elbows as though she was being rocked by an icy wind.

"It wasn't your fault that he died." Daniel grasped her shoulder and drew her to him.

"If only I'd stayed in the house. If only I hadn't run away . . ." her voice trailed off.

"Solano," Daniel looked deeply into her sad eyes. "You couldn't have saved your father from himself. How do you know that he wouldn't have gone too far this time? Maybe you wouldn't have gotten off with just a few cuts and bruises and a few broken bones . . . maybe . . ."

"In my heart I know you're right." Solano stepped away from Daniel and sat down on the sand.

Daniel noticed that she was wearing the beaded bracelet he'd seen in her jewelry box. It was doubled over to fit her delicate wrist. She was fingering the tiny beads as spoke again.

"Part of me just doesn't want to believe that he was so out of control." She looked away and watched the waves rolling into shore. "I made this for him a long time ago." She motioned to the bracelet.

Daniel smiled, then waited a few moments until the sadness had lessened in Solano's eyes.

"Sometimes I don't think I understand adults at all." He pushed a piece of hair from his eyes. "They do the most bizarre things."

"For the strangest reasons." Solano nodded.

"Like poisoning the island." Daniel shook his head in confusion. "And all for a few lousy bucks."

Daniel sifted warm sand through his fingers. Solano caressed the beaded bracelet. Her voice was a mere whisper when she finally spoke.

"Do you think the island will ever come back?" She looked seriously at Daniel.

"I suppose so. Gramps says everything heals in time."

"Everything heals in time," Solano repeated wistfully.

Daniel reached out and touched her hand.